PRAISE FOR FLOWERANTHA

If *Flowerantha* is any indication of the imagination of author Bek Castro, hang on to your seats, your hats, or whatever else you can grab. This is a visual trip into a whole different world! – Vivian Probst, award-winning author of *Death by Roses*

Castro has created a vivid land where the reader will want to escape to time and again; complete with fantastic creatures including mermaids! – Malinda Andrews, author of the *Ryder Chronicles*

Flowerantha is a very quick read! It's entertaining and I never was bored by it. The creatures were so fun to read about (I mean, T-rexes with wings? Yes, please). – Niah, blogger at Secrets Beyond the Pages

This book was a lot of fun! Exploring this new world and language was entertaining. It only took me half a page to be drawn into the story. – Kim, Goodreads reviewer

Thanks for entering my giveaway!

Flowerantha

Enjoy the adventure!

BEK CASTRO

Bek Castro

C

coppersmith

Flowerantha

Bek Castro

Copyright © 2017 Bek Castro

Printed in the United States of America

First Printing 2015

ISBN 978-0-9982661-4-5 (6x9 paperback)

Coppersmith Publishing LLP
PO Box 149
Port Washington WI 53074
www.coppersmithpublishing.com

Cover art by Leslie Bryan
Cover design by Katie Lawler
Designed by Freepik.com

To anyone who's ever pretended their backyard was a magical land and a stick was a sword.

Also to my 11-year-old self, we did it. We finally did it.

FLOWERANTHA

PROLOGUE

The liquid harp strings of a sprinkler, swinging water back and forth in the backyard, provided the escape the girls needed on that sweltering day. The sun beat down, frying the grass between the two girls' houses. The taller girl's shoulders and cheeks turned pink under the sun's intense rays, creating a stark contrast against the blue and green floral pattern of her bathing suit. Between the two of them, they had five siblings, but none were around that day.

May Lynn, a petite eleven-year-old girl with long black hair sticking to the tan skin of her back, sprinted across the lawn and through the sprinkler. But she did not come out the other side like she had the previous dozen times she had leapt through. There was a flash of pink from her bathing suit, and then she was gone. Her friend Beverly slicked her light golden brown bangs back into her chin-length hair and dug her knuckles into her eyes in disbelief. She called out, jerked her head back and forth, and tiptoed toward the curtain of water herself. When she stuck her head through, instead of seeing browning grass and her house across the yard, her eyes adjusted to the darkness of a cave. The sound of loud rushing water replaced the backyard sounds of chirping birds and humming car engines. She called for her friend again, lost her footing on the wet grass, and fell into the cave.

CHAPTER ONE

"The flowers are purple today," a woman said to her son.

Mash, a boy of about thirteen years old with a solid build, straightened out his longer-than-average legs on the tree branch he was reclining on. Pressing his back against the trunk of the tree, he looked up from the book he was reading. "What'd you say, Ma?"

His mother poked her head out of a room-sized pouch suspended from a sturdy limb. Their residence consisted of four fibrous pouches hanging from different limbs on the same massive tree. Two of the pouches were bedrooms with only a mattress and blanket in each of them. A third contained a solid floor made of wood and straw with four sawed-off cylinders of logs to sit on. And the fourth housed everything they owned heaped up in teetering mounds. Mash's sling hung higher in the tree than the other three pouches to give the privacy a teenage boy needed.

The middle-aged woman's eyebrows jumped higher on her forehead than usual, creating wrinkles on her tan face. "Ma?"

Mash wedged the book under one of his legs to hide it from his mother. The book, *Useful American Slang and Other Cultural Norms,* was given to him by his father, but anything about the *Ama Ranth*, which means "other land" in Floweranthan, upset his mother. "Ma. It's what some people call their mothers."

"You sound crazy when you use words like that, Mash. No one here is going to understand you. Please just speak Floweranthan."

Mash dangled his legs off the branch. His bare feet, which were covered in dirt, swung back and forth in the air. "What were you saying, Mother?"

"*Donch coilee*," she said in Floweranthan, meaning dark purple. "Look at the flowers. Have you ever seen them purple?"

"I do not pay attention to the flowers, Mother."

"And that will be your folly someday, Son. Look."

Mash focused on the ground far below to appease his mother. To anyone unfamiliar with Flowerantha, the scene would've been breathtaking. Fields of flowers, including all colors of the rainbow, sprawled as far as the eye could see. All different kinds lived together, interspersed with each other. The bright sun magnified the colors. To the left, a hundred yards away, was a dense forest with lush, sky-scraping green trees. A clear, small stream meandered behind their tree residence and flowed into huge lakes and rivers and waterfalls elsewhere, connecting all of Flowerantha by water.

"I don't see anything different."

His mother opened her mouth to say something, but then furrowed her brow. "More slang?"

"I *do not* see anything different."

The woman shook her head. "I do not know why those people need so many different words to mean the same thing. It is pointless and a waste of time. Why are you so determined to learn their language anyway?"

"I'm going to find a way there someday."

A crashing sound made Mash jump. The pot and lid Mash's mother had been cleaning were now on the floor of the pouch. She held the cleaning cloth between clenched fists, and her lips formed a tight line. "Enough. I will not hear another word about the Ama Ranth, do you understand? Now fetch me the bowls from storage. Please. We will be using them for the meal."

"But—"

His mother's eyes narrowed. Mash clamped his mouth shut and did as he was told. He scaled the tree with no trouble and swung himself into the hanging pouch. The bowls and other items they used every day were in the front. The day before, they had spent an hour rummaging around the different piles until they found an old book of his father's. Mash wondered why they didn't just wish for a new one, but his mother had said that wasn't the point.

People of Flowerantha could wish for any physical item. They couldn't wish to fly, but they could wish for wings. But wishes were only temporary, and no one knew how long a wish would last. They could wish for food and be nourished by it before it disappeared. If someone were to wish for a giant tree house facing the sea, the house would not last long enough for anyone to be impressed by its massiveness. In some ways, wishes made Floweranthans' lives more convenient, but they didn't make them perfect.

With three stacked bowls in one hand, Mash climbed down to the pouch where his mother waited.

His mother took the bowls and wrapped her fingers around his wrist before he bound away again. "You remember what happened with the last visitor from the Ama Ranth, right?"

"Yes, of course. He made enemies with the mermaids and tried to turn all the land walkers against them. The monsternites were doing his bidding but one day drove him away for some reason." He faced away from her so that she couldn't hear him mutter, "But not every visitor has evil intentions."

The monsternites were Tyrannosaurus Rexes with feathers covering the top of their heads, their backs, and continuing down to the tips of their long tails. The color of the feathers varied from gray to black to rust, depending on the beast. They also had powerful, leathery wings. Monsternites lived in the mountains and had kept to themselves the past ten years since the battle of the mermaids and land walkers versus the evil visitor. With only sporadic attacks over the years, the people of Flowerantha were beginning to believe the monsternites were no longer a problem.

"You do not know that. We had no trouble with those monsternites until the visitor came along. Who knows what other evils that world has." His mother's expression was grave as a deep purple shadow swept over the rainbow blooms like a cloud passing over the field.

"I'm sure it is not so bad, mother. Is it alright if I go see Nautica for a while?"

"Yes, maybe she will talk some sense into you."

Mash barely heard his mother's muttered words as he scrambled down the tree and into the meadow of flowers.

She called after him. "Be home for the meal! And be careful!"

കൈകൈകൈ

Mash followed the flow of the stream until the water opened up into a peaceful lake. He knelt down at the water's edge and slapped at the water a bit.

"Nautica."

A girl about Mash's age bobbed to the surface. Her long, blue-green hair swirled on the water's surface, almost camouflaged. Even her pale skin had a greenish glow to it. Her round blue eyes, like giant glassy marbles, stared at Mash. Her lips turned up at the corners for a second, but then her expression hardened.

"You know you do not need to do that. I can already read your mind. So can everyone else down here if they want to." Her blue fish tail slapped the water behind her. "Honestly, if you just paid more attention to what was going on here than what was going on in the Ama Ranth..."

Mash put up a hand to cut her off. "I know that, Nautica, but this is important. You might've been preoccupied reading someone else's mind."

Her eyes never left his. "You are always on my mind, Mash."

Mash continued on as if he hadn't heard her at all. "My mother was going on and on about the flowers today."

Nautica rolled her eyes. She coasted to the shore and rested her elbows on a mound of flowers and dropped her chin into her hands. Her glittering blue tail was halfway above water in the shallow part of the lake. Mash sat cross-legged next to her, and Nautica took the opportunity to lean on one of his knees.

"Do you think you will ever find a partner, Mash?" asked Nautica.

Mash's gaze remained forward. "You ask me that all the time, but you already know the answer." He peeked at her out of the corner of his eye with a half smile.

She lit up for only a second and then composed herself. Nautica moved her shoulder away from his knee but stayed beside him, following his gaze into the distance.

"You want your partner to be someone from the Ama Ranth, but you have never even met anyone from there. What if they are hideous?"

"I've seen pictures in my books—they're not hideous. They look just like us." Mash scratched his cheek. "But even if they were hideous, I wouldn't care. They're fascinating. I'm going to go there someday. I'm going to get out of here and live there."

Nautica didn't bother responding because nothing she could say would change his mind. Mash and Nautica had grown up together, born on the same day. Mash had been fixated on the other land ever since the first time he heard about the visitor when he was a young boy. Nautica would've been offended by his response if she weren't so used to it by now.

She changed the subject. "What did your mother say about the flowers?"

"Something about them being purple. She said that the flowers looked purple today." Mash adjusted his position so that he was kneeling.

The two ridges along Nautica's brow bone in place of eyebrows scrunched together to form a crease between them. "And?"

"Does that mean anything to you?"

"I do not pay that much attention to land flowers, Mash. I live underwater."

"It didn't mean anything to me either." He plucked a pink daisy and handed it to her.

Nautica traced the flower's petals with her webbed fingers. It was so lovely even if it was not meant as a gift from him.

He pointed to the edge of the petal. "Look. The edges are purple."

"What do you think it means?" She cupped the flower in her hands and inspected it closer.

"It must mean something. Maybe another visitor from the Ama

Ranth?"

Nautica dropped the flower into the water, and it floated away with the ripples created by her tail. "Shhhh. If they were not listening before, they will now. Those words will surely bring you into view in the King and Queen's *brine pool.* Anyway, it cannot be that. Olivia would know if there was a visitor here. She has been telling everyone that there is nothing to be afraid of. If someone comes, she will know what to do."

Mash plucked another flower by the stem and tossed it to the side. "Have you ever even seen this brine pool? I think it's a legend."

"No, it is far too dangerous for anyone besides the King and Queen. If anyone else were to touch the water...well, they would be in no position to tell the tale. Even Olivia cannot approach it."

"Sounds convenient."

Olivia, half mermaid and half land walker, with disproportionately long legs, webbed feet, and gills, was the go-between for land walkers and sea dwellers. Mermaids had the power to read minds, but leaving the water was complicated. For that reason, a land walker-mermaid hybrid was appointed to help the King and Queen rule both realms. Water was a powerful force, and the King and Queen had control over it, which demanded respect from the land walkers who scarcely saw their rulers.

From deep down in the sea, King Mermano and Queen Mermaida could see all their subjects from a pool hidden in their palace. The royals had been anointed by the pool's water. To anyone else, the acid water and the fumes from it would burn.

"I'm going to ask my father. People always confide in him."

"Well, that is his job," said Nautica.

Mash's father worked as a chronicler. His job was to frequent local gathering places and speak with both land walkers and sea dwellers to record the daily events of Flowerantha for historical purposes. Because of his job duties, he was always aware of all the land's gossip and news.

"Yes, it is. I'll be back in a couple days and let you know if I find out anything new. Try to do some investigating down there, too. And let me know if you hear anyone thinking about what the flowers mean. Someone has to know something they're not saying. I have to get back home. Father is probably back by now." Mash jumped up before Nautica could say anything. He took a few steps before flashing her a goofy grin. "Thanks, Nautica. You're the best."

CHAPTER TWO

On his way home, Mash decided to take a shortcut through a winding river instead of following its current back to his home.

"I wish for a bridge."

A single plank of wood materialized and clattered onto the rocky shore. It was no wider than Mash's two feet, and a crack ran through the center.

"What kind of a bridge is this?" Mash put part of his weight on the plank, and it creaked under his toes. He bounced on it with one foot, but other than a few splinters flying off into the rushing water, it seemed intact. Spreading his arms for balance, he carefully proceeded across, the heel of one foot touching the toe of the other. He held his breath in the middle as the wooden beam sagged, and a cold crest of water covered his foot. He picked his left foot up, and the crack in the wood gave way. Mash yelped as his whole body submerged into the water. Coughing, he paddled against the current and reached for a rock on the opposite shore. It took him a couple attempts to grab hold of the slippery surface. Back on dry land, Mash took long strides and arrived home soaking wet.

His mother and father perched on the log seats in their gathering pouch, speaking in low voices. "...less powerful than they used to be," said his father as Mash swung through the opening from a nearby branch.

"What is less powerful?" Mash passed his parents and plopped onto a third log stool. He lifted the bowl of liquid sitting in front of him toward his nose. Steam rose, moistening his face, and an herb scent filled his nostrils. He took a big gulp of soup and wiped his mouth with the back of his wrist.

"Mash, what happened to you?" his mother asked.

"I went for a bit of swim when I fell off a bridge."

His mother moved her hand to her mouth. "Are you alright?"

"Yes. It was more like a piece of half-broken wood than a bridge." He dodged his mother's hand as she reached for him. "What's less powerful?" he asked again.

His father leaned his elbows on the table and wrapped his hands around his soup bowl. "Son, I really do not want you to worry about this. I am sure it is nothing—mostly worried people trying to find an explanation."

"An explanation for what? I can handle it, Dad. I can help." His dad said nothing. "Do the purple flowers mean a visitor from Ama Ranth is here? I've been studying up on their culture. I'm ready."

Mash's mother pushed herself off the stool and watched the water swirl around the trunk of their tree. "The King and Queen said there is nothing to worry about. They would tell us if we were in danger. They always have been very clear with us." Although it wasn't cold—it never was in Flowerantha—Mash's mother rubbed her upper arms.

"If they knew," said Mash.

Mash's mother shook her head. "Do not forget, son. They can read minds. How could they not know?"

Mash slurped his soup, and his head snapped in his father's direction once again. "What is less powerful than they used to be?"

His father took a deep breath and stared at his rough, large hands resting on the table. He ran one of his hands through his mid-length brown-gray hair and then rubbed his beard stubble. He took another long breath. "Our powers are less powerful."

"Our powers? You mean our wishes?"

"Yes."

"That explains why my bridge I wished for didn't work. It was just a half-broken piece of wood." Mash tested what his father had just told him. "I wish for a whole loaf of bread to have with our soup."

A loaf of bread appeared on the table in front of them, but it looked like it had been left in the fire for far too long. The crust was scorched. Mash tried to grab it in one of his hands and recoiled. "Ouch! It burned me!" He held his wrist with his good hand and inspected his red palm.

"How many wishes have you made today?" asked his father.

"I've never had to count before. I could not even guess. Why?"

"Some are saying wishes are now less effective after three."

"Since when?"

"That I do not know. Days. Weeks. The purple flowers mean that the monsternites are back. And people in town are saying that when a monsternite is close by, our wishes become less and less powerful the more we wish. The monsternites haven't always had that effect on us though. Shrewtonite gave them that power."

"Shrewtonite," Mash and his mother exhaled at the same time. Silence filled the pouch—from the pressed straw on the floor to the fibers woven together on the slanted ceiling. It seemed to creep into every space like a fine mist, then rise to the ceiling, and pour out the opening and down the tree, having filled all the available space inside. The only sound that could be heard during that moment was the rushing stream in the yard, cheerful and unaware of any tension in the house.

Shrewtonite, or Ned, as he was called when he first arrived in Flowerantha, learned the language and customs quickly. He also tried to control the monsternites and became corrupt. Shrewtonite, as he was now called, lived with the monsternites and discovered a way to travel back and forth from the Ama Ranth to Flowerantha. But the monsternites could not be controlled for long. Realizing they were stronger together than apart, they drove Shrewtonite away, and he fled back to the Ama Ranth.

Mash's father broke off a piece of the burnt bread and sopped up the remaining bit of soup in his bowl. "The good news is, we don't think the monsternites know they have that effect over our wishes yet. If we make it seem like we're as capable as ever, we'll still have an advantage. If they find out...they'll be unstoppable."

Mash's mother snatched Mash's father's empty bowl and clanked it on top of her own. Before she climbed out of the pouch to clean the bowls in the water, she pointed to Mash's half-full bowl. "Your dinner is getting cold."

With unfocused eyes, Mash's mouth hung open while he processed what his father said. "I'm not hungry anymore."

"You will eat," commanded his mother.

Mash did as he was told, gulping the rest of his soup. After he finished, he leaned his head on his hand, and his knee bounced up and down.

"You are excused, Mash."

Mash swung his legs out from under the table and stacked his bowl on top of the other two. "Let me know if you hear anything else, Father." Then, he darted up the tree to his sleeping pouch.

Throwing his blanket to the side, which was stuffed with the warmest down from baby *aquasus*, or winged horse, feathers, he found his tattered, leather-bound book. Some of the pages were falling out, and some of the pages Mash had ripped out. Mash kept it together with a leather cord tied around the middle. Untying the cord, he opened the book and removed the pencil he kept in its binding.

The book contained notes about everything Mash had learned about visitors from his father and anyone else who had been alive long enough to remember stories of past visitors. Mash noted some expressions he especially liked. The word "AWESOME" was circled on one of the pages. Another page contained the names of the few visitors he had heard about through the years and anything he knew about them. There was an old man whom everyone loved. He ended up dying in Flowerantha, surrounded by many friends. Then, there was the beautiful woman, who came before his parents were born. Legend has it that she wanted more than anything to become a mermaid and died trying. Then there was Shrewtonite.

If Shrewtonite could get to the Ama Ranth, Mash thought, so could he.

CHAPTER THREE

The first thing Mash did the next morning was make the trek back to the lake to speak with Nautica. As he approached the lake, Nautica bobbed at the surface. When she saw him, she swam to shore and pulled herself all the way up onto the grass and flowers. He lowered himself onto a rock and dropped his legs into the water.

"I was thinking last night—"

"You were right," she interrupted.

"What?"

"There are visitors in Flowerantha. Two young girls." Her full green upper lip curled in disgust.

He jumped to his feet, sending a stream of water in Nautica's direction as his feet broke the surface. "I knew it. I knew it! The purple flowers. The monsternites. I can't believe there have been more than one visitor in our lifetime. I have to meet them. Do you know anything else? What do the King and Queen think about it?"

"Mash, stop." She put her fingers to her temple like she was concentrating on something.

"What's wrong?"

Her pale skin lost the green tinge and became even paler. "Sit down here."

"What? What is it?"

"Sit! Please." Mash scrunched up his face but did as he was told. He kneeled with one knee in the ground next to Nautica, leaving the other foot planted and at the ready.

"I am in your father's head right now." She paused, and her blue eyes, which were darker with apprehension, stared into Mash's confused, but still soft and inviting, gray ones. "A monsternite is near your house. Flying over it right now, but it seems to be slowing down."

Without a second's delay, Mash pushed off with his foot and stood. "I have to go back."

"No!" She grabbed him by the legs so that Mash fell down. He struggled, but she pulled him into the water. Merpeople were stronger than land walkers; and in the water, land walkers didn't stand a chance. Mash tried to break free from Nautica's arms, which were wrapped around his chest. "Mash, listen. Just let me think!"

He relented for a moment. "Tell me they're safe."

"I am trying. Hold still."

"I promise I won't run. Just put me back."

"No, I do not trust you. Just hold still." She touched her temple again with one finger. "The monsternite is not stopping. They are safe."

"How can you know that? You can't read monsternites' minds."

"There is a rider. I have never heard of a monsternite being ridden, but there is a rider on this one. He is looking for the visitors. He does not care about your parents, but he is considering destroying them just in case." Mash tensed up, and Nautica tightened her grip. "But he is leaving." Mash relaxed, but Nautica remained tense.

Mash cleared his throat. "Um, Nautica. You can let go now."

"I think you should stay here for a while. Until we know for sure it is safe."

"If you're keeping me here, then I want to talk to Olivia and see if she knows anything else about the visitors."

"Fine. Let me find you a sparklesphere, and we will go talk to her." Nautica splashed around and peered into the water, but she couldn't locate any spheres nearby. She threw up her hands and said, "I wish for a sparkleshere."

"Don't waste those. You only have three," said Mash.

"Only three good ones, as I hear it. You are lucky that was not my fourth wish. I could have gotten you a sphere with a leak in it."

Mash ran his hand over the sphere to find the puckered area that expanded to an opening big enough for him to crawl into. He stopped halfway with only his torso in the sphere. "It wasn't your fourth, was it?"

Nautica laughed but didn't answer. She held the seam of the sparklesphere and pushed Mash the rest of the way in by his feet.

There were a few means of transportation for land walkers of Flowerantha to visit the sea dwellers underwater. Sparklespheres were the most convenient. One could find a sparklesphere floating around in a shallow part of a calm lake. The sparklespheres were oblong, glittering, person-size bubbles, but they were unable to be popped. Although they were the easiest form of underwater travel to come by, they had their drawbacks. Sparklespheres were only ideal for short journeys unless the passenger could find a place to refill the air. They were also hard to steer—sometimes merpeople would help by pushing the bubble along. Otherwise, it could take the passenger a lot longer to get where they were going. But with a mermaid guide, there was no easier way to get around.

The two sank for a while as fish flitted by, their scales shining in the darkness. The sparklesphere bumped into the top of an enormous glass structure. The palace resembled a crystal hive that acted as a prism and emitted rainbow-colored lights, with dozens of openings on every side and on top. A deep field of coral surrounded the hive like a moat. Mermaids came and went through the openings nodding to Nautica as she pushed the sphere through one of the openings.

"Here are Olivia's quarters." Nautica grasped the puckered part of the sphere to slow it down outside of a room with frosted crystal walls. Nautica knocked on the door and threw Mash a skeptical glance with a brow ridge arched.

"Who is it?" Olivia's voice boomed even more so underwater than on land.

Nautica poked her teal head through the doorway. "Olivia, pardon me. Shall I come back later?"

"No," said Mash. He motioned for her to go on.

Olivia craned her neck to look around Nautica. "Who is with you?"

"We need to tell you something important. Or, Mash does." Nautica stepped away from the door and pushed the sparklesphere into Olivia's view.

"Hello, Mash." Olivia nodded to him.

"Hello, madam. Olivia. Your highness. It's a pleasure." Mash bowed his head in return.

"You may call me Olivia. I am not royalty."

"Thank you, Olivia. I was hoping I could—"

"Wait." Olivia held up her hand. "It will be easier if you do not speak." Her eyes bore into Mash's, and she waited to absorb his thoughts. Mash obeyed and stared back, his lip twitching as he concentrated. "You would like to help with the visitors."

"Yes, more than anything."

Olivia squinted her eyes and pursed her lips, but then her face softened. "And you are wondering why the monsternites were by your home. Your family is safe. I will tell you what the monsternites are planning, because if I don't tell you, I know that Nautica will read my mind and tell you later anyway."

Nautica averted her eyes.

"What did they want?" asked Mash.

"You have heard that Shrewtonite's castle is under construction. And that the monsternites were looking for *russet* workers and forcing them to make the castle livable for monsternites. That was the work of only a few monsternites, led by Shrewtonite's right-hand beast, Scorso. But that is not the reason the monsternite flew by your home."

"Is it because of the visitors?"

"The monsternites have sensed the visitors, and they are rallying again. But they do not know what the visitors look like, which is how we would like to keep it. We do not know what the monsternites would do if they caught them, and we would like to keep these girls safe."

Nautica made a disgusted sound.

"And Nautica's reaction is why I chose not to tell anyone. After

Shrewtonite, most Floweranthans are going to have distrust for any new visitors. These, however, are not a threat. I have a young soldier-in-training on a quest right now to return them home as quickly as possible before anyone notices they are here. He left earlier today."

Mash trembled with excitement, and the sparklesphere vibrated around him. "I can help. I need to help."

"I know, but I have already told you too much. I will speak to the King and Queen, and if they agree, you may help, too."

Mash bounced in the sphere. "I can do it. Can we meet with them now?"

Olivia's lips pursed together and turned up at the corners. "Yes, I suppose it would do for them to meet you. Then with their consent, you can leave tomorrow at first light. I have a place you can stay for tonight."

Olivia held out her hand to gesture for them to leave her alcove. Once in the hall, she kicked her legs to propel herself past them. The gills that had been covered by her silvery hair puffed out as she breathed under the water. Her muscular arms and large, webbed hands and feet propelled her through the water. She wore nothing, but her scaly skin looked more like a wetsuit than bare skin.

Nautica followed, pushing Mash's sparklesphere ahead of her. Mash turned his head and peeked at her with a wide grin, finding Nautica's face creased into a frown.

"I could get used to this service."

Nautica slapped the sphere, and Mash leaned back as much as he could in the tight space and put his hands behind his head.

When the three entered the throne room, Olivia halted and bowed. "Your majesties."

Nautica floated beside the sparklesphere and mimicked Olivia's movement while Mash sat up at attention and crossed his legs.

A flurry of activity revolved around two majestic-looking merpeople at the center of a great room. The King and Queen sat on gilded thrones. The Queen's long golden hair, secured by a crystal crown, swirled around her pale pink skin. The King had a full golden beard to match his thick hair. Their tails shown gold or green, depending on how the light reflected on them. The King, Queen, and Olivia stared at each other for a moment, communicating without words, before the Queen spoke.

"Hello, Olivia. More business to attend to?" Queen Mermaida's voice flowed like a lazy river. With the Queen's smooth, delicate skin, she did not look much older than Olivia, although she was old enough to be her mother.

"Two more citizens are now aware of the female visitors. They wish to help the young soldier-recruit find the passageway back to the Ama Ranth."

"No one else was to know." The vibrato of King Mermano's bass voice shook the room. "Can these two be trusted?"

Mash bobbed his head, but waited for the King's attention to be directed towards him to speak. "Yes, your majesty. I believe I am perfectly fit for the task." He followed up his bold remark by averting his eyes and laying a hand over his heart.

Olivia kicked her legs so that she stood between the sphere and the King, probably to discourage Mash from speaking out of turn again. "He considers himself an Ama Ranth expert, and the mermaid, Nautica, is his best friend. They will protect each other, if need be. And I will accompany them along the way. The young recruit, Bushraal, and I can train them in self-defense. Bushraal's father was highly skilled."

The Queen looked skeptical, but concerned.

The King was not swayed. "Yes, his father's skills were unmatched, but a party that large is sure to raise suspicion. If the monsternites find out about the visitors..." He didn't finish his thought. "And they are just girls. We need to protect them until we can get them back where they came from."

"I agree completely," said Olivia.

"And you will accompany the children the whole way, Olivia?" asked the Queen.

"Yes, I will." Olivia's chin tilted up as she waited for their final decision.

The King sat in silence for minutes on end, leaning forward in his throne, and Mash's muscles ached with the effort of trying to stay so still.

"I will trust your judgment. But no one else can know. We do not want another war to start from this. That is all, Olivia."

"*Graciyoo*, your majesties," Olivia thanked them as she bowed and exited the room, and Nautica and Mash mirrored her again.

The mermaid, the hybrid, and the land walker traveled across the lake, staying near the surface in an effort to avoid meeting curious merpeople. Land walkers traveling underwater with mermaids was not uncommon, but Olivia said that she did not want to take any chances or answer any questions. Olivia surfaced, and Nautica gave the sphere one last push. The bubble bobbed up and down in the rippling water. They were floating in front of a small waterfall.

Olivia tipped her head. "There's a cave on the other side of the waterfall. You can climb up the side and slip in. And you will be pleased to know, Mash, that the very cave you will sleep in tonight was where the visitors entered Flowerantha."

"Are you kidding me!" Mash exclaimed in disbelief as he pushed his way out of the sparklesphere and scrambled onto the shore. He stood up and reached his arm through the falling water into the emptiness of the cave. "Thank you," he said.

Olivia nodded and splashed back into the water. Nautica put her arms up as she prepared to dive.

"You're leaving, too?" His eyes were wide and pleading.

She hesitated. "No, I do not have to go yet. Go check out your magical cave," she said sarcastically. "I will wait here. Let me know how it is."

Mash beamed and lodged one bare foot beside the waterfall. He stuck his arm in again, then his other arm, then hoisted his body up.

"It's dark," he called through the noisy water.

Through the din, he heard Nautica say, "Get used to it, land walker. Are you afraid of the dark?"

"Of course not." Mash waved his hand through the water. "I think I'll be alright. Bye, Nautica."

"See you in the morning, Mash."

He heard a splash, and he was alone. Mash ran his hand along the cool stone walls. It smelled a little musty, but not too unpleasant. The water drowned out any other sound from the outside. Mash was separated from the rest of the world by that wall of water. The whole of Flowerantha could burn to the ground. A herd of monsternites could be at war just on the other side. Seasons could change, which never happened in Flowerantha, and Mash wouldn't have known. The endless pounding of the water and the trapped feeling prevented him from falling asleep at first. He lived in a tree house without a door. He was not used to being this enclosed. To avoid the spray from the water, Mash lay on his side at the back of the shallow cave. He bent his elbow under his head to use as a makeshift pillow. In his mind, he wished he had a blanket, but he was careful not to say it out loud for fear of what mangled mess might appear. Eventually, the rhythmic sound lulled him into slumber.

࿔࿔࿔

When Olivia called his name the next morning, Mash peeked his head out of the side of the waterfall, holding his hand in front of his face to guard it from the spray and the brilliant sunlight. His eyes squinted, and his hair was disheveled. "Is it time to go?"

"Yes."

"I'll be right out."

"I will meet you on the land." She swam to shore and hoisted herself up over some rocks.

Mash jumped into the water and paddled to where Olivia was seated on the land. While she filled him in on the plan, Mash patted the water with his hand. "Where is Nautica?"

"Nautica is in school. You will have to relay the plan to her later, if you would like her to join you," said Olivia.

Mash nodded. "I would."

"Remember, the King and Queen do not want to create chaos—or worse, a war—if they do not have to. They are still wary after the last visitor, so discretion is of the utmost importance."

Mash nodded again. "Believe me, I have no one to tell."

"After you eat something, I will take you to meet Bushraal. He should not be far yet."

Mash squinted one of his eyes from the sun and picked a piece of grass. "Do you have only three wishes, too?"

Olivia tilted her head and frowned. "No, mine are still unlimited as far as I can tell."

"Then can you wish for breakfast?"

Olivia let out a throaty chuckle. "Of course."

Mash and Olivia ate on the bank while Mash questioned Olivia on everything she knew about the Ama Ranth. Just as they finished eating, Nautica popped up in front of them. "I heard the plan. I would like to go, too."

"You may accompany Mash. We will stay close to the water as much as we can. We will have to separate when we go through the woods on our way to meet Bushraal, but we can reconnect with you on the other side." Olivia paused and redirected her attention at the water. "No. Not now."

"What is it?" asked Mash.

"I am needed on official business. This journey will have to wait."

Mash shook his head. "It can't wait. Nautica and I can go. Just tell me the way."

Olivia hesitated. "I will join you as soon as I can, or I will find someone else to meet up with you if I cannot. Hurry to Bushraal's home so that you can travel the rest of the way together. He will teach you how to defend yourself and protect the visiting girls. He is younger than you, but you must listen to him. He will be a good guide. I must go. Good luck, Mash and Nautica. I will be there as soon as I can."

CHAPTER FOUR

For much of the day, Mash walked along the water while Nautica swam beside him. They tried to keep their conversations light and their heads clear in case any merpeople happened to be listening from below. The terrain stayed the same most of the way—clear blue lakes lined by fields of colorful flowers, some of them a dark, ominous purple, and random shady trees and bushes filled with berries. Mash reached for one of the bushes and grabbed as many berries as he could at once. He gave some to Nautica, and then they took turns trying to throw the berries into each other's mouths.

In the afternoon, it was time to split up. A river veered off one way while a dense forest was the last thing between Mash and Bushraal's home. Nautica grimaced and shifted her gaze from side to side. "Why has Olivia not come yet?"

"I'll be fine," said Mash. "It's just a little walk through the woods. After I meet up with this Bushraal, we'll find some water and continue to the mountains."

"Please be careful. I will be in your mind the whole time."

"I will. Thanks, Nautica." He pivoted on his heel.

"Mash." She held out her hand. Her blue eyes seemed to have grown even bigger and more watery than usual like she was about to cry.

He knelt down and squeezed her outstretched hand. "I will see you soon."

As Mash plunged into the woods, his bare feet landed on a sharp stick. He winced and picked his foot up. No damage. "Good. I don't want to waste a wish." He followed a narrow dirt path covered by a leafy canopy. "I hope I know where I'm going."

He found a large stick on the ground that he used to club tree branches on each side of him when the path became too narrow or almost disappeared. Leaves rustled as he brushed by them, and sticks snapped beneath his feet. After walking almost all day, Mash collapsed in a heap and leaned his back against the nearest tree. "Just a quick rest," he said to himself. "I want to find Bushraal before the sun sets."

Mash pushed his foot forward and watched as he displaced the dirt, bark, and other debris. With his hand, he made a pile of dirt and then patted it down. To finish off his little creation, he found a twig and stuck it in the top of the mound.

"Maybe I'll get to the Ama Ranth after all." He swung his hand at the little hill he had made, destroying it.

The woods grew darker, and Mash still had a ways to go before he reached Bushraal's home. Getting up from his spot against the tree, he continued on with his walking stick in hand. Mash hummed to pass the time as he swung at the brush on either side of him. When he finished humming one song, he paused. He heard the sounds of twigs breaking in the distance. Out of the corner of his eye, Mash saw a flash of white from the trees. He spun around and saw another flash of white in the opposite direction.

"Who's there?" His voice trembled. "Or what?"

Another flash of white crossed his line of vision, and Mash ran. His large walking stick slammed into tree trunks and became tangled in a web of vine-like branches. Mash tugged at it for a second, but then abandoned the stick. He continued to run, but his foot caught a root, and he tumbled to the ground. His hands and face were now covered in dirt, and the woods would only get darker. The leaves above hid most of the remaining sunlight.

"I wish for a torch."

As a cone-shaped piece of wood with a blazing top materialized in his hand, a great, white form dropped to the ground in front of him with a thud. The beast was taller than Mash with gray-white hair covering its entire body except for mustard yellow fur on its snout. A menacing smile spread across its elongated, pointy face. It looked like a sloth but did not move like one. These animals, called *gamboges*, were quick and agile. The gamboge opened its mouth and swung an arm at Mash—an arm that was as long as the rest of the body itself. Three long, white daggers protruded from the end of the creature's hand. Mash dodged the sharp nails inches from his face and shoved the torch at the outstretched arm. The gamboge screamed, and Mash shielded his ears as best he could from the piercing sound. A branch creaked from above. Another gamboge with a smiling face perched on the tree above the first gamboge. It blinked its beady, black eyes and crouched like it was ready to pounce. Mash crawled backward, supporting himself with his free hand while swinging the torch with the other.

"You better stay where you are." He pointed the torch at one gamboge and then the other one. He stood up and backed away, one cautious step at a time. The gamboge on the ground matched his steps and advanced toward him. The one in the tree crouched down lower and licked its lips with its long tongue that wound itself around like a snake. Their hair was like straw, like maybe if lit, it could catch on fire and extinguish the animal in seconds. But it kept the animals dry when the waters rose. Mash took another step, but his heel made contact with a fallen tree. He lost his balance and flailed a bit, shaking the torch at the gamboges. Seeing his weakness, the gamboge in the tree leapt off of his branch. Mash, unable to do anything else, covered his face and stuck out the torch, bracing for impact.

Instead of plowing into Mash, the airborne gamboge screeched and fell to the ground. The other gamboge froze for a second, and then climbed a tree and swung with his long arms from tree to tree in the opposite direction until he was out of sight. Mash stood over the gamboge on the ground.

"*Deraino*," said a voice in Floweranthan.

Mash spun around to find a boy maybe a year younger than he was and a few inches shorter. The boy wore a dark-colored tunic and sandals. He carried a bow in one hand and an arrow in the other that matched the arrow sticking out of the gamboge. His blonde hair was wild and wavy and hung to his eyebrows, framing piercing blue eyes that could be seen even in the dark.

"Graciyoo. Can I see your bow?" Mash reached out his hand, but the boy snatched it away.

"What are you doing in the woods alone and unarmed at night?"

"I am armed." Mash held up his torch, which was now a stick with glowing embers on the end.

The boy frowned. "These gamboges sleep during the day and eat at night. It is not safe to be wandering around."

Mash kicked some dirt at his feet. "I wasn't exactly wandering. I'm looking for someone called Bushraal. Do you know him?"

The boy notched the arrow against the bow but kept it pointed at the ground. "I am Bushraal. Who are you besides a lost russet?"

"Well, I'm not lost...I may be a little lost, but I am a russet if that's what you want to call us poor people. Olivia sent me. The King and Queen's royal messen—"

"I know who Olivia is."

"Right, well, I'm here to help you on your quest. She said you would train me to help protect the visitors." Mash peered around Bushraal. "Are they with you?"

"I do not need help, especially from a *russet*."

"Look, I knew your name. Olivia trusts me, and I promise I'll be useful. I know a lot about the visitors."

Bushraal sighed. "Very well, but I am not putting away my bow just yet. The visitors are waiting at the edge of the forest." Bushraal wished for a wheelbarrow in which to carry his prey, and Mash helped him load it before they stomped through the woods.

With Mash's long legs, he passed Bushraal and called over his shoulder. "So with being a soldier in training, is that bow something you get issued, or did you have to wish that up?"

"You know too much about me already, russet."

"It's Mash, actually, and now you know as much about me as I know about you."

"I doubt that. The weapon belonged to my father, and I use it for hunting food. I am not in the training program yet, but I hope to be in a few years."

Mash snorted. "So Olivia sent a boy, not a soldier, or even a trained recruit, on this quest? Why?"

"I am more than able. My father was in the royal army, and I will be in the army soon, too. He trained me to use a bow and arrows. It is as much a part of me as my own arms." To make his point, Bushraal drew back on the bowstring and sent the arrow straight through a fruit hanging from a tree.

"Awesome," said Mash. "And now you can teach me."

Bushraal stopped and shot him a quizzical and annoyed sidelong glance.

"I've been brushing up on my Ama Ranth slang. I hope to go there someday."

"No one in Flowerantha has ever gone to the Ama Ranth," said Bushraal.

"Except for Shrewtonite."

Bushraal's fists tightened around the wheelbarrow hands, and his arms tensed. "You should go work for Scorso. I hear he is giving the rights of passage to whoever builds his castle."

"If I believed that, I would go, but I don't trust monsternites. My father said that those people are being used as slaves."

Bushraal grunted. "That is probably true. Evil beasts. Still, it seems like a good place for a russet."

Mash fumed, but his anger disappeared when they came to the tree line where two girls in strange clothing stood waiting. He froze with his mouth hanging open, and Bushraal brushed past him with a shove. Bushraal walked between the girls and turned halfway back to Mash. "Coming?"

Mash strode up to the taller girl and stuck out his hand. "Hi, I'm Mash. I'm here to help you get home."

The girl squeezed his hand, and he jerked it up and down. "I'm Beverly." She tucked her straight, golden-brown locks behind her ear.

The shorter girl with the long black hair put her hand out next and took his hand without squeezing it, and he flapped hers up and down, too. "May Lynn." She withdrew her hand and held it with her other hand.

"My house is not far now," said Bushraal, leading the others back into the woods.

Mash positioned himself between Bushraal and the girls, forcing him to move to the other side of the group next to Beverly. Mash walked sideways as he directed all his attention at the visitors. "How did you get from the Ama Ranth to Flowerantha? We still have not been able to figure out how transportation works between the two lands."

"Ama Ranth? Is that like a combination of America and Earth?" asked Beverly. Mash and Bushraal showed no recognition in their faces, and Beverly's cheeks colored as she shrank into herself. "It sounds like it."

"It means 'other land,'" Mash helped. "So how'd you do it?" He galloped sideways with a goofy grin on his face as he waited for their answer.

May Lynn fidgeted with a thin, stretchy band around her wrist. "We were playing in my backyard, running through the sprinkler, and I kind of fell through the water into the cave behind the water-fall."

Mash's expression was blank, and Beverly added, "Do you have sprinklers here? They're like a metal thing that shoots water into the air. They're for watering grass or just running through."

He sounded the words out one by one to process them. "You were playing in the water at home, and you ended up in the water here." He gestured to their bathing suits. "That would explain your, uh, clothing."

Beverly's bathing suit was blue with large flowers over it, and May Lynn's showed a strip of her stomach and was pink with smaller scale flowers and a thin ruffle along the top.

Beverly pulled the stretchy fabric, making a tent shape over her stomach. When she let go, the fabric snapped back in place. "Yeah, it's really weird walking around some unknown place in just a swim-suit."

"I am surprised Olivia did not offer you something of hers," said Bushraal, bringing the attention back on him.

Beverly giggled. "Well, she wasn't wearing anything."

"I do not believe she wears clothes underwater, but she does when she is doing business on land."

"Oh." Beverly's sunburned face grew even pinker when she blushed.

"I could wish you something, but wishes only last so long." Bushraal shrugged as much as he could under the load of the wheelbarrow and tossed his head to clear a lock of hair out of his eyes. "My mother may have something acceptable."

"Do you have any brothers or sisters?" May Lynn's shoulder brushed against Bushraal's arm, and he veered away from her slightly.

"I do not."

The girls nodded but didn't speak.

"I don't either," said Mash. "I guess that means we have something in common, Bushraal."

Bushraal smirked.

"What about you?" asked Mash to the girls.

"I have a younger sister," said May Lynn. "Her name is Kelly."

Beverly didn't say anything until Mash's eyes flicked in her direction a couple seconds later. "I'm the middle child. I have two older brothers, Steve and Rob; a younger brother, Willy; and a younger sister, Mary."

"Large family. I would want to have a large family," said Mash.

Beverly heaved a sigh. "It's exhausting." She cleared her throat. "Hey Bushraal, I don't want to be a wuss, but it kind of hurts walking through the woods barefoot." She tiptoed over the brush, holding a tree for support.

"My apologies," he said. "I wish for two pairs of sandals for May Lynn and Beverly."

Beverly squeaked as a pair of leather straps wrapped around her ankle and a sturdy bed of leather replaced the poky sticks under her feet.

"Thank you, Bushraal," said May Lynn.

Beverly lifted her foot to inspect the sandal. "Yeah, thanks. That's much better."

"*Deraino*," he said. "You are welcome."

At the clearing, an amazing sight greeted the group. Two great trees stood in the middle of the field with Bushraal's home built high up in their branches. The main part of Bushraal's house was made of wood and built around the branches of a tree. It was cylindrical and two stories high with two rows of thin windows and a pointed spire roof. From the house was a bridge to another tree and a wooden deck built into the branches of the second tree.

"How many of you live here?" Mash gazed in wonderment. His entire home could fit twice easily into Bushraal's.

"Just my mother and me."

Beverly clasped her hands in front of her. "This is the coolest place I've ever seen."

"Where is your father?" asked Mash.

"Dead."

May Lynn lay her hand on Bushraal's shoulder.

"It is alright. It has been years. Now I just want to be a soldier like he was. I want to be a man he would be proud of."

A petite woman popped her blond head out of the treehouse door. She piled her wavy hair on top of her head and stepped outside onto the bridge. "Cerulean, Bushy! Who are your friends? Come on in and have some tea, everyone."

Bushraal gritted his teeth. "I asked you not to call me that, Mother."

The woman shrugged and continued pinning her hair up.

"Graciyoo, madam. That's very kind," said Mash.

Beverly and May Lynn followed Mash up the wooden staircase that led to the front door of Bushraal's tree house. The stairs creaked on each step.

"Do not mind the stairs. They are very old, but very safe."

From afar, the dress Bushraal's mother wore appeared to be an ordinary, but pretty green and white dress; but up close, the details were amazing. The bodice of the dress was made of thick pieces of grass woven together like a basket. Cream-colored flowers with soft petals covered the skirt and shoulders of the dress.

"I really like your dress," said Beverly.

"Graciyoo." She straightened out her skirt, and a couple of creamy petals fell through the slats of the bridge and floated to the ground. "If you are going to blend in, you will need to wear something like this. You may borrow some of my things. I am not sure if we will be able to find anything to fit..." She eyed Beverly. "...but at least you will be clothed. Come on in."

Inside the door, Bushraal pointed to Mash first. "This is a russet whose life I just saved. Apparently, Olivia has sent him to join me on my quest as my apprentice. We are to return these two visitors, Beverly and May Lynn, to the Ama Ranth." Bushraal's mother covered her mouth and nearly choked on the hairpin between her teeth. "Please do not tell anyone. Part of my quest is to make sure no one knows they are here."

"Our quest now." Mash bowed his head. "Hello, madam. My name is Mash."

Bushraal's mother giggled. "No need to bow, Mash, but graciyoo. I could get used to being treated like royalty more often. Please, sit down. I will make you all some tea. I would love to talk to some girls for a change."

"Go on in," said Bushraal. "I'm going to prepare the gamboge meat."

Everything inside Bushraal's house was made of wood. The trunk of the tree cut right through the center of the round room. Beyond that was a round kitchen table with four chairs surrounding it. To the right of where they entered was a small wooden bed with blankets pulled taut and tucked in the sides. To the left was a ladder leading up to the second floor. Bushraal's mother bustled into the kitchen and took a pitcher down from the shelf and set it on the table. "I wish for donkleberry tea." The pitcher filled with thick black tar instead of tea. "*Maoompy!* What is this?"

Mash tipped the pitcher and stuck his finger in the black goop. "Have you possibly used more than three wishes today?"

"Of course," she said. "Does everyone not use more than three wishes?"

"Yes, normally."

"Well, if you wait here, Mash, Bushraal can wish up something to drink with our meal. Girls, if you follow me, I can find you some clothes."

Beverly and May Lynn followed Bushraal's mother up the stairs and into her bedroom.

Mash picked up the pitcher from the table and tipped it back and forth while the gooey black liquid crawled from one edge to the other. He put his nose down into it and sniffed. It was fruity and fragrant, like donkleberry tea should be, but the consistency and color were all wrong. He set the pitcher down on the table when he heard the steps outside creaking.

"Where are my mother and the visitors?" Bushraal carried a slab of wood heaped up with thick hunks of pink meat.

Mashed pointed up. "Up the stairs."

Wiping his hands off on a cloth, Bushraal's sandals clapped the floor as he ascended the stairs. Bushraal wandered into the bedroom with Mash on his heels. The second floor was dedicated entirely to Bushraal's mother. A giant canopy bed stood against the back wall with a dressing table on another wall. Three bamboo wardrobes lined up side by side on the third wall to the left of trap door in the floor and across the room from the bed. Bushraal's mother was digging around in a trunk at the foot of the bed. Bushraal sat backwards in the dressing table chair, and Mash stood nearby.

"Have you no decency, boys? There will be ladies changing in here. Please go downstairs and find something to drink."

Bushraal's cheeks turned pink. "I am simply making sure you do not pick anything too fussy. They need to blend in and look like Floweranthans."

"Bushraal, I am a Floweranthan. They will look just like me." She continued digging in her trunk while the boys hovered in the background. She pulled out a green and purple knee-length dress. The top was made up of large, shiny leaves with bunches of lilacs on the neckline. The skirt was made of layers of evergreen leaves with more lilac bunches at the bottom. She held the dress up in front of Beverly. "You may be able to squeeze into this. I wore it when I was pregnant with Bushraal. I was absolutely huge back then."

"Mother!"

Beverly's face went crimson. She took the dress and mumbled. "Yeah, I'm really tall. Thanks." She then disappeared behind the dressing curtain beside the wardrobes.

Mash fiddled with some of the beauty instruments on the dressing table. "You've met Olivia. Now, she is really tall. You're not too terribly tall at all, Beverly."

A polite but forced laugh came from behind the curtain. "Yeah, I guess."

Bushraal's mother left the trunk open but rose from her knees to open the middle wardrobe. "Here are some more things I kept from when I was younger in case I ever had a daughter. I want to keep the nicer things just in case, but I am sure we can find something in here."

"Anything is fine," said May Lynn. Bushraal shot her a sympathetic glance, and she returned it with a sweet smile.

Bushraal's mother selected a dress with a bodice full of orange berries and a slim, knee-length skirt of leaves and a scattering of orange mums. "Here, try this one." She handed it to May Lynn. Taking the dress, May Lynn joined Beverly behind the curtain. Mash picked up a brush with coarse bristles and ran his finger over it.

"That is gamboge hair," said Bushraal.

"I know that."

When the girls walked out from behind the curtain, Bushraal stood, and Mash clunked the brush back down on the table. The orange complemented May Lynn's tan skin. Beverly's dress was a little shorter than intended, and she tried to smooth down the lilacs that were askew from being stuffed in a trunk for twelve years.

"These look better than expected." Bushraal's mother stood up from the bed and smoothed down the berries at May Lynn's waist and straightened the flowers at the bottom of Beverly's dress, tugging it down a little. "Really, other than the length, you look lovely in this."

"You both look beautiful," said Bushraal. The girls fidgeted.

"You look like you belong here." Mash's words sounded kind, but his expression was unsure. Maybe the visitors weren't so different from Floweranthans.

Bushraal's mother glided down the hall and led the group downstairs. "Bushraal, please wish us something to drink with our gamboge meat."

"I wish for five goblets of mead."

She frowned, but no wrinkles formed on her face. "You are a little young for mead."

"This is my first real quest. I think it is cause for celebration." He clinked his glass with Mash's before taking a swig.

Mash gulped his drink and coughed as the bitter liquid stung his throat. "You didn't poison mine, did you?" He coughed again and wiped his mouth.

Bushraal laughed and slapped Mash on the shoulder. "That is how it is supposed to taste, russet. Drink up."

CHAPTER FIVE

The next morning, Mash woke to a quiet house. Bushraal snored in his bed, and May Lynn's black hair peeked out of the blanket she was sleeping under on the floor near him. He tried to sit up, but grabbed his head in the process. "Ow." He tossed the blanket off of him and leaned his elbows on his knees. Using his hands to block the light streaming in the windows, he cradled his head. Standing up, he saw Beverly sitting at the table with her feet bent underneath her. He kept one hand on his head as he shuffled to the table to join her. "Cerulean." His voice was raw and scratchy.

"Hi." She futzed with the lilacs at the bottom of her dress.

Mash took a seat across from Beverly and propped one leg up on the chair next to him. "How long have you and May Lynn known each other?"

"Three years. Ever since her family moved in next door."

Mash nodded. "I don't have any neighbors. I don't know how much longer I'll have a house either if the monsternites get to it."

Beverly fluffed her skirt and readjusted her position. "Those monsternite things sound really scary. I want to get out of here as fast as possible just so I don't have to run into one of them."

"They are scary, but you have nothing to worry about with me. I will not let anything happen to you or May Lynn," Bushraal said from across the house. He appeared behind Mash's shoulder.

Beverly smiled, propped up her elbow, and rested her head on one of her hands. "Hey Mash, what is that word you said before when you came over here?"

"Cerulean?"

"Yeah, what does that mean? Isn't it a color? I think I've seen that word on a crayon."

Mash furrowed his eyebrows. "What's a crayon?"

"It's something you color with." Beverly cupped her hand with her fingers touching like she was holding a crayon and pretended to write on the table.

"Like a pencil," said Mash.

"Yeah, but with colors."

Mash nodded, considering the idea. "I should like a crayon. Anyway, cerulean means 'hello' in Floweranthan."

"Ser-OO-lee-uhn," she said, syllable by syllable. "And Bushraal, your mom said something in Floweranthan last night when she was trying to make tea. Oompa loompa something?"

Bushraal scrunched his nose and chuckled. "Maoompy. That is—" He paused, reaching for an English equivalent and made a circular motion with his hands. "If something disgusts you. My mother says that one quite often. She likes things clean."

"Gross," Mash helped. "It means gross."

Beverly winced. "No wonder she doesn't like me. I'm pretty messy."

"She does like you, I think. She seems to like May Lynn," said Bushraal.

"Of course."

He opened his mouth to clarify. "I can see how May Lynn would be quite likable, but you are too. You made me laugh just then, and that is not an easy task. I believe my mother is concerned because you are from the Ama Ranth. The other land. Nothing good has come from there lately."

"What happened?"

Before he could answer, the floor creaked on the other side of the room, and May Lynn sat down on the last free chair, rubbing her eyes.

"Cerulean!" said Beverly.

"Um, hi," said May Lynn. She and Bushraal exchanged fond yet shy glances.

"That means 'hello.' Mash taught it to me."

When Bushraal's mother woke up, she used up her wishes on a large breakfast of eggs, bread, fruit, sugary pastries, and anything else she could think of. Bushraal groaned.

"You feel as sick as I do, huh?" asked Mash. "Except I'm starving."

"You two should not have drunk so much last night." His mother passed him a plate with two eggs on it.

Bushraal sniffed and turned away from the table, holding his hand over his mouth. "I will just eat the toast. I am really not feeling so well."

"Suit yourself." She scraped the eggs onto Mash's plate across from her.

"These are delicious, madam," said Mash. "Better than my mother could wish up actually." Bushraal clapped his hand over his mouth again, this time to mock Mash's sincerity.

Bushraal excused himself from the table, grabbing a piece of toast as he went.

"So girls," Bushraal's mother said, pouring some milky liquid in each of their glasses, "I must say, it is so fascinating to have visitors in my own home. Are there any questions we can answer for you?"

May Lynn shook her head.

Beverly put down the fruit that she had been picking at—a round fruit the size and texture of an orange except it had a blue rind surrounding orange flesh. "I don't know if I'm supposed to ask this, but what happened to that Shrewtonite guy? How did he get away? Olivia didn't tell us much."

Mash leaned forward, nearly knocking his own glass over. "It's still a mystery. A group of land walker hunters saw him dive into a small pond, not even as tall as a man. Then land walker soldiers showed up and started questioning the hunting party, but they couldn't explain it. After that, many people went to that pond to try to pass through it like Shrewtonite did. But they just ended up muddy."

"Time for some training. Then we must depart. It is a long way to the mountains," said Bushraal. He propped his foot up on a chair and laced up his sandal. Bushraal had changed his clothes from the previous night. The night before, he had worn a navy blue linen uniform shirt with a V-neck and sleeves rolled up to his elbows and breeches for pants. Mash had assumed the shirt was his father's due to the size of it. Bushraal now wore a stiff woven bamboo vest and shorts, this time with a sky blue linen army shirt underneath.

Mash stood up and faced Bushraal.

Bushraal frowned at Mash's feet. "Where are your shoes?"

"I don't have any. I hardly ever wear shoes."

Bushraal shrugged, but his mother rose and squeezed Mash's arm. "You need shoes to get out of these woods. I have an old pair of my husband's somewhere. Let me see if I can find them."

Bushraal's eyebrows came down so far they covered half his eyes. "Do you really want to give father's shoes away?"

"Bushy, I miss him, too, but he has been gone a while now. We cannot have you boys wasting wishes on things I can give you right now." She retreated up the ladder to her bedroom and came down with three pairs of leather sandals. "Girls, I brought a couple pairs for you, too. I noticed you no longer have the ones you wore last night."

As Mash put on the sandals, Bushraal said, "Are you ready now? Anything else you need of my father's?"

"Maybe he should take a weapon, too," said his mother.

Before Bushraal could make a biting retort, Mash put his hands up to refuse. "I'm okay, madam. Thank you for the shoes, but I will worry about weaponry later. My friend Nautica can secure me something from the mermaid kingdom if I need it."

"Just take it. You need something to practice with anyway." Bushraal spun on his heel and was down the stairs before his mother could come back with his father's sword.

When Mash found Bushraal in the yard, he was shooting arrows one by one into a tree, hitting almost the same spot each time. Without looking over, Bushraal asked, "Bow or sword? What would you like to start with?"

"I think I have sword fighting handled already." Mash swished the sword through the air and mimed thrusting it at an enemy as Bushraal still stood poised with an arrow balanced on his bow.

Bushraal lowered his weapon. "Right. We will start with the sword."

Mash had been doing everything wrong. From the way he held the sword even to the way his feet were positioned, Bushraal corrected it all. Mash was receptive at first, but it didn't take long before he grew tired of the young boy's impatient instructions. They sparred and Bushraal scolded until they were both sweaty, red-faced, and fed up with each other.

Bushraal wiped his forehead with his sleeve. "You will not become a soldier, but you know the basics at least. We will head out now."

Talkative Mash said nothing, and he continued silently fuming all the way up the stairs, through the door, and even when May Lynn asked how it went.

"Are you leaving now?" asked Bushraal's mother. When Bushraal said that they were, she embraced each of the children, but lingered in her son's arms longer. "Please be safe, Bushraal."

Mash noticed tears in Bushraal's eyes, but he blinked them away. "I will make you and father proud."

"You already do, Son. Just come home safely. *Erosea*, Bushraal."

"*Erosea*, too, Mother."

To Mash's dismay, Bushraal kept them in the forest for most of the day. He explained that he thought it would be safer than being exposed along the water. Although he wasn't as sure of this particular route, he was confident that it would bring him to his destination anyway.

Hours later, they reached the edge of the woods, which bordered on a slow-moving river. Nautica was waiting, leaning her elbows on the shore with the water moving past her.

"Cerulean," said Bushraal.

Mash pushed past Bushraal. "Nautica! Hello!"

"Cerulean," she said. "It is a pleasure to meet you, Bushraal."

"The pleasure is mine." Bushraal locked eye contact with Nautica for a few seconds until she smiled, and then her eyes flicked in Mash's direction.

"A sloth, Mash? You were almost attacked by a sloth?"

He smirked. "It was a gamboge. They're faster than you may think."

Her attention settled on the two young girls next, and her smile shrank. "Are these the visitors?"

Mash guided each of the girls forward with his hands on their backs. "This is Beverly and May Lynn." May Lynn gave a silent wave and then stared down at the flowers on her own dress.

Beverly clasped her hands together. "It's so exciting to meet a mermaid. I love your hair."

Nautica barely acknowledged the girls before she addressed Bushraal again. "To the castle then?"

"Yes, to the castle."

The boys walked right on the water's edge with the girls next to them while Nautica swam against the current beside them.

"Have you heard from Olivia?" asked Mash.

"No, I have not seen her since we left. No one can tell me where she is either, so this official business of hers must be pretty secret."

Bushraal's stomach growled.

"Was that you?" asked Beverly.

"We just ate before we left," said Mash.

"You ate. I had nothing," said Bushraal.

"I don't think you should waste a wish on food just yet. Maybe we'll find some berries if we keep walking. Or eat them off of May Lynn's dress." Mash plucked a single berry from her shoulder.

She slapped his hand away. "Hey!"

"I am not that desperate. Those berries are fifteen years old. I will be fine." He touched his bow. "When you have a bow and arrow, you do not need to waste wishes on food at all. I can wait." His stomach growled again, and he put his arm around himself in an attempt to stifle it. "Let's keep walking." His voice softened as he cast a glance at Nautica. "Or swimming."

The sun blazed high in the sky, but the group felt comfortable, not too hot. Flowerantha's temperature was always perfect. The terrain changed the further they walked. The never-ending garden of flowers became sparser and sparser with larger expanses of grass between each bloom. The mountains were in view and getting bigger. Soon, Nautica could not go on with them.

"I guess this is where we part again," said Mash.

"I will find us food before we go. Wait here," said Bushraal. "Is there anything you would like, girls? Nautica? A bird? Squirrel? Gamboge perhaps?"

Nautica hid a smile behind her hand. "No, thank you. I do not eat meat. But you may. I am not offended by it, depending on the meat."

Bushraal's cheeks reddened. "I will not return empty handed," he said and spun on his heel.

Mash burst out laughing and held his stomach. "Even I know mermaids don't eat meat, and I don't pay that much attention."

Nautica sent a stream of water flying at him with her tail. "Be nice, Mash. He is trying."

"Um, Mash," said May Lynn. "The flowers are changing colors. Is that normal?" The flowers that dotted the grass around them changed from vibrant pinks and yellows to a pale sky blue.

Wiping tears out of his eyes from laughing, Mash looked at the flowers with disinterest. "Yes, it's normal. They change colors all the time."

When Bushraal returned and they parted from Nautica, he brought them back to the tree line to set up camp for the night. "Gather all the long sticks you can. We can make a shelter for the girls, and I will wish for some blankets." Mash, May Lynn, and Beverly got to work picking up fallen branches and snapping low ones off of trees while Bushraal wished for a knife and sawed some of the thick boughs.

Soon, they had constructed a comfortable escape for themselves in the form of a lean-to made out of sticks and a crackling fire nearby. Mash wished them each a blanket, and the girls huddled around the fire to eat.

"Before you sit down, Mash, we need to have another training session." Bushraal held the knife out to Mash, handle first.

Mash grumbled as he wrapped his fingers around the knife handle.

Bushraal stepped out of the way. "Try that tree. I cleared some branches for you." He pointed to a tree directly in Mash's line of sight but far enough away to present a challenge.

Mash arched his arm back and let the knife fly in the direction of the tree. It hooked to the right and rustled into a bush. The girls giggled.

Bushraal gestured to the bush. "Well?"

Mash ground his teeth together and stomped towards the bush. He reached his arm into the middle of the bush while the sharp thorns hidden by the leaves raked across his skin. His arm was striped with bright red lines when he repositioned himself to try again. This time, he overcompensated, sending the blade far to the left. The girls held back their giggles. Mash's shoulder sagged in defeat, so Bushraal retrieved the knife for him.

Giving him the knife, Bushraal said, "We're not eating until you hit the tree."

On his fifth try, the knife grazed the side of the tree, shaving a piece of bark off. Mash looked to Bushraal for approval, but also daring him to say that wasn't good enough.

"Close enough. We can eat," said Bushraal.

Beverly cheered, and May Lynn clapped her hands.

Without waiting for it to cool down, Mash grabbed a stick with meat on the end from the fire and chomped into the blackened meat. He waved his hand in front of his mouth to try to cool it down as he chewed. The meat was tough and salty and drier than he would've preferred. But it was food, and it tasted like a prize after hitting the tree with a knife.

Beverly picked at some of her meat. "I love that there aren't any bugs here. If we were at home right now, we would be getting eaten alive by mosquitoes."

Mash's gray eyes widened. "Eaten alive! I had no idea it was so dangerous in the Ama Ranth."

"Oh. No, that's just a saying. I mean, it is dangerous in some ways. They do suck your blood."

Mash's mouth opened, and his inquisitive expression turned into a horrified one.

"No, no. I'm not explaining it right. Mosquitoes are just annoying. They'll just make you itchy." She held out her arm to Mash. "See? I have a mosquito bite right there."

"That tiny bump?" He sounded disappointed.

"Yeah, that's all they do pretty much."

May Lynn brought her knees to her chest, hugged them, and rested her head on her arm.

"You look sad," said Bushraal.

"Not really sad. More scared. I was just thinking about my family and wondering if I'll ever see them again."

"You miss Kelly? I thought she bugged you," said Beverly.

May Lynn frowned. "Yeah, but she's still my sister. You miss Steve, don't you?"

"What is a Steve?" asked Mash. He poked the fire with his stick.

"He's my oldest brother. My other brothers are annoying, and my sister and I don't have much in common, but Steve and I are buds."

May Lynn lifted her head off of her knees. "I don't think Rob and Willy are annoying."

"That's 'cause they both have crushes on you. I don't think Kelly's that bad."

"Our moms and dads probably think we've been kidnapped." She hugged her legs tighter. "We need to get home."

Bushraal went to pat her leg, but instead he clasped his hands in front of him. "I am sorry you are scared. We will keep you as safe as possible."

"I wish we all could go to the Ama Ranth," said Mash.

Beverly reclined on her side next to the fire and arranged the blanket over her. "This may sound weird, but I didn't even think about how worried my parents would be."

"My parents waited so long to adopt me and Kelly. They would be crushed if they lost one of us. I don't even like thinking about it."

"Unlike mine who have four replacements if I go missing."

May Lynn shook her head. "Don't say that. Your mom and dad would miss you, too."

"Yeah, I know." Beverly used a blanket to wipe a tear dripping down the side of her nose before anyone could see it, but Mash noticed.

May Lynn yawned, and Bushraal pointed with the stick he had been poking the fire with. "You two can sleep in the shelter. I will stay out here and keep watch." The girls wrapped the blankets they had been sitting on around themselves and ducked under the array of sticks and lay down.

Mash lay down on his side in front of the fire. "Do you want me to take a shift?"

"No, I do not think I will fall asleep tonight."

"If you say so." Mash yawned, closed his eyes, and nestled his head into the crook of his elbow.

CHAPTER SIX

The sound of Beverly yelling woke Mash up some time later. It was still dark, and the last curls of smoke from the dying fire did not provide any extra light. The smell of the campfire filled his nostrils. He felt a hard kick to his leg.

"Ow!" He sat up then and rubbed his thigh where Bushraal had kicked him.

"Get up! The waters are rising. We need to get somewhere high. Now!" Bushraal grabbed May Lynn's hand and took off running through the woods.

In the dark, it was only moments before Mash could no longer see the two of them. Beverly waited a second for Mash to get up while she marched in place in the ankle-deep water.

"Hurry, please hurry," she chanted.

Realization hit Mash, and he slapped his forehead while the water swirled around his still-sitting body. "The flowers. Blue means the water will rise. My mother was right."

Bushraal appeared again with fire in his eyes. "Beverly, leave him behind if he is going to sit there." Bushraal grabbed Beverly's upper arm, and Mash pushed himself off the ground to follow the others. Bushraal darted through the woods toward the tree line. The water was over his knees, and their pace slowed.

"Where are you going?" yelled Mash.

"I remember a hill close by. It is large enough that we will be safe from the water," called Bushraal over his shoulder.

"We'll never make it!" Mash surveyed the trees surrounding them. "How good are you at climbing trees?"

No one answered as they sloshed through the water inching closer and closer to their waists. Mash reached out and grabbed the person closest to him. "Beverly, can you climb trees?"

Her face was panicked, and her chest heaved with the effort of running through water. "Yeah, I do it all the time. We have good climbing trees in my backyard."

"Good. Pick a tree and climb it."

Bushraal stopped and panted. His eyes were wild. "He is right. We have to climb." He created a step with his hands to boost May Lynn up onto the lowest branch, and then he jumped to pull himself into the same tree.

Beverly stretched her long legs as she planted her foot onto branch after branch and reached for the next one to pull herself up. The water lapped at her feet. She was out of breath, and the branches above were getting thinner and thinner. "How long do we have to stay up in these trees?"

Bushraal called back from his tree. He was standing on one limb with his hand on May Lynn's back on the next branch up. "The water should stop rising now. We are high enough. But it will not go back down until the sun rises. We need to stay here for a couple hours at least."

Mash scaled the tree nearest to Beverly without any effort at all. She was trying to find a comfortable position for her hands and feet. He shouted to her, "Are you going to be alright for that long? I think I could climb over there if I needed to." The branches of their trees overlapped, but he would be hanging by twigs to get from one tree to another.

"No, don't do that. I'll be fine. It's not like I'll fall asleep now."

෧෧෧

As the sun rose, the waters subsided, like someone had pulled the plug in a bathtub. Bushraal jumped down into the ankle-deep water and offered to find food. "Stay here until the water is gone. I will return shortly." He splashed through the water away from the group.

Mash climbed down his tree and then directed Beverly and May Lynn how to climb down theirs. When May Lynn was low enough, she put her weight on Mash's shoulder, and he reached up to guide her the rest of the way down.

Brushing off her dress, she asked, "How much longer do we have to go?"

"Bushraal said we will be able to make it all the way to the monsternite castle tomorrow."

"I'm not looking forward to that." May Lynn shivered.

"I wish I could say it was going to be easy, but I don't think it will be. We don't even know for sure if there is a passageway to your land in the castle. But it is our best guess." Without thinking, he rubbed her arm to smooth out the goosebumps that popped up. "I don't know about Bushraal, but I have never been inside the castle. I wouldn't know what to look for."

"You'll get us home somehow, right?" asked May Lynn. She was still leaning against him. Her warmth made him tired as he realized how little sleep he had gotten the night before.

"Yes, we will find a way to your land."

Beverly cleared her throat, and May Lynn backed away from Mash as Bushraal splashed back to the group. Only he wasn't alone. Four white horses with wings walked beside him.

The girls' jaws dropped.

"Impressive," said Mash.

"Is that a Pegasus?" asked Beverly. "With um, duck feet?"

"Aquasus actually." Bushraal knelt and touched the animal's foot. "When its hooves touch the water, they transform into webbed feet. Once the water dries up, they will turn back into hooves."

May Lynn pet the creature's mane, and Beverly hugged herself and crouched down at a safe distance.

"Why do they need webbed feet?" asked Beverly in a hushed voice.

"Well, they need some advantage over monsternites." Mash

crossed his arms over his chest, and then uncrossed them and stuck his hands into the pockets of his leaf shorts, doing anything with his hands to avoid petting the aquasus.

Bushraal smirked. "Are you afraid of it?"

Mash crossed his arms once again. "Of course not. I've just never ridden one."

Bushraal ran his hand down the length of the aquasus, stroking its soft, downy fur. "They are used mostly by the merpeople."

Bushraal tossed him a mushroom. "I brought something to eat."

Mash bit off a big chunk of one of the mushrooms and chewed. Bushraal and the girls watched him. "What? Should I be worried about these mushrooms?"

"The aquasus said it could be eaten," said Bushraal.

Mash swallowed. "Well then, let's go."

"Have you ever ridden an aquasus?" Bushraal asked the girls.

They shook their heads. "I've ridden a horse," said May Lynn.

"But they don't fly," Beverly pointed out, still from her crouched position.

"It is perfectly safe. Even mermaids can ride aquasi, and they do not have legs."

Beverly stood by an aquasus. She draped one arm over its back, just behind its wings and the other over its hindquarters. She lifted one leg, but her dress hindered her from lifting it very far. She hiked up her dress as much as she dared but then didn't have any free arms to hoist herself up with. With a little whinny as if the aquasus was giggling at her, it knelt down so that Beverly could climb onto its back. May Lynn's aquasus wasn't quite as helpful, so Bushraal formed a stirrup with his hands so that May Lynn could step in it and swing herself up. The four aquasi lifted into the air, and both the girls let out a shriek.

Beverly crouched down on the aquasus' back, squeezing her eyes shut.

May Lynn's long, black hair flapped like a flag behind her. She inhaled the sweet air. "It's beautiful."

When Beverly finally allowed herself to open them, her eyes widened at the beauty of the scene below them. The colors were overwhelming from above. Crystal blue water reflected rainbow sparkles back at them like a diamond. Lush green grass was peppered with bright flowers. And tall trees right below their feet. "There are so many flowers here. It must rain a lot."

"Rain? No, it does not rain. It does flood sometimes, like last night, whenever King Mermano feels the earth needs it," answered Bushraal. Unlike Beverly, he sat up straight on his aquasus, confident and comfortable being airborne.

"Look!" May Lynn pointed into the distance.

Mash moaned.

A monsternite was headed straight for them. Bushraal grabbed his bow and loaded it, and Mash wished for a sack of knives.

Bushraal craned his neck. "Are you sure knives were the right choice?"

With no weapons of their own, the girls were helpless. The monsternite hovered by them for just a second and chomped his teeth in their direction, but he continued on his path without stopping. Mash reacted anyway and chucked a knife at the beast. It lodged into its backside, and the beast let out an ear-splitting roar. The monsternite still did not turn around, but the threatening sound was enough to spook Beverly's aquasus. It bucked, and Beverly slipped from its back. Mash reached for her, but his maneuver caused him to lose his grip on the aquasus and plummet right behind her. They was falling through the sky. His vision was impaired by his watery eyes, and he was too scared even to yell for help.

CHAPTER SEVEN

Mash tried to twist around to see the ground beneath him, but he could only peek over his shoulder. The wind whipped past him, whistling in his ears. His back slapped against the branches of trees, which slowed his fall. He fell through one canopy of leaves and twigs, then another, and finally into a bush. The prickly branches of the bush felt like hundreds of pins violently jabbing into his skin. He cried out, and tears stung his eyes.

"Don't be such a wimp, Mash," he told himself. He blinked and wiped his dirty hand over his eyes.

Moving each of his limbs one by one, he tested if anything was broken. Everything moved with little pain besides some noticeable tenderness where bruises were forming. It was mostly his back and neck that ached. He pushed himself up to his feet and groaned.

"Wait, where's Beverly?" His stomach turned, and his aching muscles tensed. He called her name, but his voice was hoarse. The wooded area where he had fallen bordered a small lake. He dropped to his knees at the edge of the water and scooped a handful of water into his mouth.

"Beverly!" he called again.

Something brown floating down the coastline caught his eye. He ran down the sandy beach and pulled the object onto the grass. It was the burlap sack, and it still held five of the throwing knives he had wished for. He swung the bag over his shoulder and gasped as the cool, damp fabric hit his warm back. Then he angled his hand over his eyes to block the sun as he scanned the lake and the surrounding area. "Beverly!"

He heard a faint whimper behind a large boulder. Hurrying behind the boulder, he ran right into a hunched over Beverly.

"There you are," said Mash. "You're soaking wet. Did you land in the lake?" He put his arm around her shoulder, but he had nothing with which to cover her.

"You're here! I was scared I was all alone." Beverly's chin quivered, and she wiped her nose on her wrist.

"Of course I'm here." He dropped the sack and rubbed both her arms.

Beverly shivered and hugged herself. "Did you fall, too? Your shirt is ripped."

"I did. You and May Lynn aren't the only ones who had never ridden an aquasus before. I should stick to what I'm good at—climbing trees." With a move of his arm, he winced. "I wasn't as lucky as you though. I landed in a bush and scraped up my back." He rotated so that she could take a look.

Beverly touched the torn leaves to move them to the side as Mash flinched. "Sorry. You are pretty scraped up."

"Can you just rip it off? It hurts to have anything touching my back."

"Um, sure." Beverly sniffed and lifted the leaves from his back and tore it until the shirt was in two pieces.

"I'm going to dip in the lake, then we can get to the castle. Hopefully we'll see Bushraal and May Lynn along the way." Mash sighed as the cool, refreshing water eased the heat of his back. Beverly knelt down in the grass to wait.

"Hey, are you and Bushraal enemies or something? He seems mad at you all the time. I don't know if I'm supposed to trust you or not."

"You're supposed to trust me," said Mash. "I don't know what his problem is with me, but Olivia wouldn't have sent me on this quest with him if I wasn't trustworthy."

Beverly shivered again and plucked a few blades of grass. "Yeah, that's what I figured."

With only his head above water, Mash swung his arms and made little whirlpools around himself. "Are you alright? You still look scared."

Beverly dug her fingers into the grass and yanked out a handful this time. "Are you kidding? Of course I'm scared! I almost got eaten by a flying dinosaur. And that was after I fell off a flying horse with duck feet. And I'm wearing PLANTS. I was kind of having fun at first, but where I come from, it's not dangerous like this. The most dangerous thing I have to worry about is not getting hit by a car when I cross the street on my bike."

Mash cocked a half smile. "I don't know what any of those things are, but if that's all you have to worry about, then I would really like to go there."

"Maybe if I knew how to use a weapon, I could've done something," said Beverly. "At least I wouldn't have been a sitting duck like I was."

"Maybe I can help you with that." Mash stepped out of the lake with water dripping off everything, from the leaves on his shorts to the brown hair on his forehead. He went over to the sack of knives, pulled out two, and handed one to Beverly. "We can both practice our knife throwing."

"It's heavier than I expected. I guess I'm used to the toy swords my brothers have. And steak knives we use to cut our meat at home."

"Yes, I guess they fly better when they're heavy. Here, hold it like this." He grasped the knife in his palm with his index finger along the top of the handle in order to aim, just like Bushraal had shown him. Drawing his arm back, he propelled the knife directly into the tree he was aiming for.

He whooped. "I did it! Now you try."

He watched as Beverly held her knife. Adjusting her grip, he squeezed her hand closed around the handle and then separated her index finger from her fist to move it into position. "There. Now, make sure your arm starts out straight and ends up straight."

"Follow through. Got it," Beverly muttered. She threw the knife, and it whizzed right by the tree trunk and clattered against a root.

Mash chuckled. "Not so easy, right? But your form looked good, I think. Let's try again." She swung again and managed to lodge the very tip of the knife into the tree. "Wonderful! You're a natural. You caught on a lot faster than I did, at least."

Beverly nodded and pulled the knife out of the tree. "It's kind of like throwing a softball."

Mash raised an eyebrow.

"Softball. It's a sport," she said. "Something you play. Never mind."

"Those knives were my first wish for the day. Only two to go. Hopefully they will last us long enough." He stuffed two knives in each of his pockets. "You can keep the last one."

Beverly felt her dress for any pockets. "Where?"

Mash analyzed her options with a finger on his chin. "Here, let's do this." He knelt at her feet and cut off a length of leather cord that was tied around her ankle. Sticking the end of the cord through part of the woven grass that made up the foundation of her dress, he tied the knife in place at her right thigh. Then, he arranged a lilac bunch over it. "Be careful not to cut yourself."

"Yeah, no kidding. I wish I had pockets." She smoothed the lilacs over the knife in an attempt to cover it more. "Speaking of wishes, have you always had three per day? And why don't I get any?"

He tilted his head. "You know, I don't know why visitors don't get wishes. I guess it's in our blood. We used to have unlimited wishes; but lately with the monsternites around, we are only able to use three wishes a day. If we use more, they're basically useless."

"That's not fair! You used to have all the wishes you want and now you only have three?"

Mash sighed. "The monsternites have more power than they should."

Mash and Beverly walked the beach in silence as their hair and clothes dried from their dip in the lake. The sun beat down on their shoulders, but it felt more refreshing than sweltering. The sand was also cool and didn't scorch their toes as they displaced it with each step.

"What is the Ama Ranth like?" asked Mash.

"You're going to have to be more specific."

"How is it different from Flowerantha, specifically?"

"Well, it was pretty hot there when we left, and it's nice here."

"Is it always hot there?"

"No, definitely not. Especially not where we live. Sometimes it gets really cold and snowy. But I suppose other places are hot all the time. Like Africa or South America. And other places are cold all the time, like...I don't know, like the North Pole, I guess."

"I'm going to get there someday."

Beverly shrugged with her palms up. "Why would you want to leave? Your family is here."

"I just don't feel like I fit in here. Yes, I have a family, and yes, I'm best friends with a mermaid—you don't have mermaids there, do you?"

"Unfortunately not. At least, not that anyone knows of. I don't think your mermaid friend likes us though."

"No, she probably doesn't." Beverly's eyebrows knitted like she expected a different answer. "As close as we are, I hate to say it, but she knows I'd leave her and this place at the first chance I got."

"Bushraal seemed pretty impressed with Nautica. It kinda seemed like he likes May Lynn, too."

Mash's expression turned to stone. "I got that impression as well."

Beverly crossed her arms tighter. "May Lynn will be okay, right? I mean, she'll be safe with him at least? Bushraal's like a knight, right?"

Mash's head snapped in her direction. His tone was rushed as he said, "He says he's going to be a soldier *someday*, but that doesn't mean he knows everything. He has no idea what the russets in the castle are going through just to get a chance at a new life."

Beverly chewed on her lower lip.

Mash ran his hand through his hair. "He just has some silly notions about russets. He doesn't respect us for some reason. I can't figure him out."

Beverly nodded. She kicked the sand as she walked, sending puffs of debris into the air with each step. They had been walking shoulder to shoulder, but Mash drifted to the left, away from the water and away from Beverly's side. Their silence lasted as long as the beach did. After what felt like an hour or more, they were walking on grass.

"I'm sorry for bringing it up," said Beverly, quiet enough that Mash could barely hear it.

Mash laughed through his nose. "I guess deep down I don't respect the soldiers either. Or wannabe soldier in Bushraal's case."

Beverly started to say something, but Mash covered her mouth and froze.

"What?" she said through his hand.

He motioned to get down, and Beverly flopped to the ground with a thud.

A small creature maybe half the height of May Lynn that was light green in color and looked like an alien with round, animal-like eyes and bug-like antennas hobbled toward them. The creature wore a maroon suit made out of velvet.

"Cerulean!" it said.

"Oh, it's just a *zomp*." Mash stood, brushed the dirt off his knees, and waved. "Cerulean."

"Cerulean, my name is Tumpske."

Mash introduced them both.

"Wow, you just appeared out of nowhere," said Beverly.

"Magic, girl." Tumpske snapped his fingers. He disappeared again and reappeared on a tree branch above them. "So you be trying to get to the castle, eh? Maybe I can help with that. For a price. I know a shortcut." The creature crossed his arms.

Mash's pleasant expression turned serious. "What's the price?"

He held up one finger. "One wish."

Mash jutted his jaw out.

"Those are valuable now, doncha know?" said Tumpske.

"Yes, I know," said Mash. "I think we can get to the castle on our own."

"But would you not like to get there...quicker?"

"That would be nice, but that's a high price to pay." Mash crossed his arms and looked at Beverly for an opinion. She shrugged. "Alright, I will pay it."

Tumpske opened his maroon suit coat to reveal all sorts of odds and ends that would not fit undetected under his jacket if not for magic. Some of the artifacts were tools, such as wrenches and hammers. He also carried a couple pocket watches, a pearl necklace, a few mason jars sticking out of pockets, and vials of liquid attached by thin strips of fabric. He untied the bindings around a telescope and took it out.

"This is what we need. Magic scope. We will be able to see castle right through trees." Tumpske put his eye up to the small end of the telescope.

"Can I see?" Mash reached out his hand, and Tumpske let him look through the scope himself.

Tumpske swiped it down from his eye after a second and clutched it to his chest. "That's enough, Mister Mash. It be very special. You dunno how to use it. I will help ya."

"Did you see anything?" asked Beverly.

"I actually did. I saw the castle far away beyond the trees. We better get moving."

"Yes, we better, Mister Mash," said Tumpske. "Follow me." The group wound through the forest, not sticking to any path, but stopping for Tumpske to check the scope and walk whichever way he pointed. After about a half hour, Beverly's stomach grumbled.

Mash touched his own bare stomach. "Was that you or me? I'm getting hungry."

"That was me," said Beverly.

"Tumpske, are we getting any closer? This part of the forest looks very familiar."

Tumpske looked up at the overhanging trees. "What makes you say that, Mister Mash? Much of the forest look alike. It all be trees."

"Yes, I know, but I remember those two trees specifically. The one is growing through the trunk of the other one. That is pretty unusual, don't you think?"

Tumpske ignored the question. "We can eat real soon." Another half hour passed with the three of them stomping through the forest, and Tumpske stopped once again to use the scope. "Ah yes, the castle is much, much closer now. Care to see, Mister Mash?"

Mash snatched the scope up and squinted through it. His eyes widened. "Actually, the castle does look closer now. Do you want to see?" He handed it to Beverly, who also put it up to her eye while she closed the other. Beverly shrugged and handed it back to Tumpske.

"What the matter, Miss Bev?" asked Tumpske.

"Sorry, I don't mean to complain, but I'm getting really hungry now."

"We've made some good progress. We could stop now, couldn't we?" asked Mash.

"One more stretch." said Tumpske.

Mash lay his hand on Beverly's shoulder. "Can you make it?"

"Yeah, yeah, I'll live. Let's go."

A little into their last stretch, Beverly hurried to catch up with Mash, who had gotten far in front of her since she was dragging her feet and lagging behind. Once she was in stride with Mash, she elbowed him and put her hand up to shield her mouth. "Aren't those the trees you were talking about earlier? We've passed them at least two times now, but I didn't want to mention anything until I was sure."

Mash halted and stepped in a circle, surveying his surroundings. "Tumpske, what is the meaning of this?"

"Of what, Mister Mash?"

"Let me see that scope again."

"If you think that's a good idea."

Mash held out his hand and waited for Tumpske to set the scope in his palm. Before Mash put it up to his eye, he turned it over a couple times and then shook it.

"Hey now! Don't break it!"

"As if that's possible." He gazed through the scope again. The castle appeared even closer, so close that he couldn't see the whole thing at one time. "This isn't right."

"Um, Mash." Beverly poked him in the arm.

"What is it?"

"He disappeared, and I don't know where we are anymore."

Mash took the scope away from his eye. His mouth hung open as he rotated around in a complete circle. "I know exactly where we are. The zomp must have sent us here to put us off course. And we couldn't be more off course." Mash stomped through the field of flowers toward a tree in the distance.

Beverly hurried after him. "How far are we from the castle?"

"Remember where we started, at Bushraal's house?"

"Yeah."

"Farther than that."

Beverly fell to the ground and sprawled out on her stomach with her arms and legs splayed and her face down in the flowers.

Mash stopped and put his hands on his hips. "What are you doing?"

"Dramatically collapsing, what does it look like? This is what I do when I don't know how to handle something."

Mash let out something that sounded like a laugh-sob. "Does it ever work?"

"Not usually, but it makes me feel better."

"Come on, let's find something to eat, then we'll start up again. The long way." He offered her a hand and pulled her to her feet.

CHAPTER EIGHT

"So where are we?" asked Beverly.

Mash kept his gaze forward and locked on the tree. "This is where I live."

"Where?" Beverly rotated her head to the left and the right.

Mash pointed at the tree. "In the tree. You see those pouches hanging down? It's not as nice as Bushraal's, but it's home. My bedroom is a lot more comfortable than his floor though."

"Now I have to meet your parents?" Beverly tugged at the bottom of her dress and arranged her bangs over her forehead.

"You look fine. You look like you could live around here. Which reminds me." He grabbed her arm and faced her. "Don't tell my mom you're from the Ama Ranth.

"Why not? I'm really not a good liar."

"Then let me do the talking. She doesn't trust visitors and hates when I talk about the Ama Ranth. She would be furious if she knew I brought a visitor to our home."

Beverly's eyebrows shot up. "What about your dad?"

"My dad would love it, but he can't know either."

"Okay. I'll just...not talk."

Mash trod through the flowers, dragging his feet and trying to think of something to tell his parents. He considered claiming she was his girlfriend and reached for her hand before he thought better of it. Digging his hands into his pockets, he tried to come up with a better idea. Next to him, Beverly fidgeted, tucking her hair behind her ears, straightening various lilac bunches on her dress, and sighing every few seconds. Mash was just as nervous, for different reasons, and couldn't do anything to comfort her.

The tree loomed in front of them, and Mash tilted his head back and shielded his eyes against the sun. "Hey ma, are you home?"

A voice came from above. "Mash? Mash!" The lowest pouch swayed as his mother poked her head out. "You are safe! And I told you not to call me ma. Where is your shirt?" His mother was halfway down the tree before she noticed Beverly and frowned. "Who is this?"

"I ripped my shirt. I will get a new one from the storage pouch." Mash lifted his arm to present Beverly. "This is Bev...vy. Bevvy."

His mother looked from Beverly to Mash, and then back to Beverly. "Cerulean, Bevvy."

"Hi. Cerulean, ma'am." Beverly waved a little and bit down on her lower lip. The three were silent for seconds on end, and Beverly had begun pushing at flowers with her big toe.

Mash cleared his throat. "Bevvy was one of the workers at the castle until she was rescued."

"So that is where you were." His mother wrung her hands. "Shortly after the monsternite flew over our tree, a messenger came and told us you were safe, but you would be away for a while. Of course, I did not accept that explanation until he said you were in Olivia's care."

"We were supposed to be," mumbled Beverly.

Mash coughed. "Olivia took good care of me. I was with Bevvy, and I offered to take her home, but then we ran into a zomp who zapped us back here."

Mash's mother stuck out her hip and placed her hand on it. "And where is home, Bevvy?"

Mash opened his mouth to answer, but Beverly spoke first. "I live in a treehouse in the forest. It's all made out of wood. Your home looks much cozier though."

"Cozy, yes. We think so." Mash's mother's eyebrow went up, creating a single forehead wrinkle. "Would you like to see it?"

Beverly clapped her hands together. "Oh, yes please."

When Mash's mother wasn't watching, Mash put a hand on Beverly's back and thanked her silently with his eyes. She smirked and nodded as she hoisted herself up into the tree.

Mash's mother grunted as she pulled herself up onto the next branch. "Bevvy, tell me, how were the conditions in the castle?"

"Um, pretty scary."

"You will have to tell us more once Mash's father returns from town, if it does not upset you too much."

"Sure."

They climbed into the gathering pouch, and Mash's mother gestured for them to sit down. Mash watched Beverly to gauge her reaction. An open-mouthed grin was spread across her face as she took it all in. She really was pretty when she smiled.

"We really can't stay long, mother," said Mash.

"Stay for the meal. Then you can be off again as long as you promise to return home quickly, Mash."

"Yes, mother." He didn't know if he could keep that promise, but his mother would not take any other answer.

Unlike Bushraal's mother, Mash's was not one for making conversation. Mash and Beverly sat at the table, sipping fruit juice and staring past each other while Mash's mother bustled around the small space and prepared the meal. It wasn't until Mash's father climbed the tree and popped his head into the pouch that anyone spoke.

"Is the meal ready? Oh hello." Mash's father made eye contact with Mash the second after he saw Beverly. His bushy eyebrows were raised. Mash was sure he knew. The fact that he said "hello" instead of "cerulean" gave him away.

Before his father could say anything more, Mash introduced Beverly. "Dad, this is Bevvy. She was one of the workers in the castle, and I was helping her get home before we got sent here by a zomp." He said it all in one breath without pausing.

Mash's father nodded slowly.

"I thought you would have many questions for her," said his mother.

He sat down between Mash and his mother, facing Beverly. "No, no questions. I'm sure she's plenty overwhelmed already. I'm just glad she's here. Safe."

Beverly blushed and hid her face behind her cup.

When his mother's back was turned, Mash mouthed the word "thanks" to his father who tipped his head in response.

After the meal, which Mash's father filled talking about his day so that Beverly wouldn't have to, Mash gave Beverly a tour of the other pouches that made up their home. He first took her to the storage pouch, where he dug around and showed her things she wouldn't see back in the Ama Ranth. Then, they climbed up even higher in the tree to his pouch while his mother leaned out as far as she could to watch them from the gathering pouch.

Beverly crawled into his room first and situated herself on top of his blanket with her legs tucked under her. Mash sat on the edge with his feet dangling outside of the pouch.

"It really is perfect here," she said, running her fingers over the stiff fibers of the wall. "I would love if I had a bedroom outside in a tree like this. It would be a perfect place for reading books."

A smile tugged at the corners of his mouth. "That's exactly what I do here." He pulled out his Ama Ranth journal from under the blanket and held it out to her. "That's where I write down everything I know about your land."

Beverly carefully opened the book to the first page and turned the next page using only two fingers. "Wow, you've really done your homework."

He leaned in closer with their heads almost touching to read what she was reading. He was about to point something out to her when he heard a deafening roar that shook the pouch. He grabbed onto either side of the opening so that he wouldn't fall out.

"Is that what I think it is?" Beverly cowered and pulled at his blanket to hide under it.

His mother screamed and ran to the back of the gathering pouch, making it rock back and forth.

"Stay here!" yelled Mash. He leapt to his feet and drew one of the throwing knives out of his pocket. "I wish for wings!"

He began to float, his body parallel to the ground. Kicking his feet like a frog, he wrapped the fingers of his free hand around a branch to propel himself forward.

"Mash, no!" His mother hung out of the pouch and reached her arm up to him.

Below, his father shot off an arrow in the direction of the monsternite, but the arrows simply lodged into the outer layer of the beast's thick skin.

"Mash, get back inside!" His father broke his eyes away from the beast for a second and set his gaze on his airborne son.

"No way, Father." Mash tilted his weight and flew closer to the beast, but something made him stop short before making a move with his knife.

A man was perched on the back of the monsternite. There was a rider, just like what Nautica saw when the monsternite first flew over his house days ago. The monsternite's giant wings beat in Mash's direction, blowing his hair and sending him backwards toward the tree. Mash leaned forward to try to reclaim the space. The man, who had short strawberry blond hair and manicured mustache complete with a beard shouted something that Mash couldn't hear at first. The beast veered sharply, and the man threw himself down against the scaly back to prevent himself from falling. Now the monster's enormous head and beady eyes focused on Mash.

"Give us the visitor!" the man shouted again.

"Mash!" Mash's father was already out of arrows. "I wish for a poleax." A large axe on top of a long pole appeared in his hands. Charging at the beast, who was still airborne, he swung the weapon as hard and as high as he could without letting go of it. The sharp metal gashed the monsternite's heel. The monster roared, bucking his rider off. The hot air from the monsternite's breath threw Mash off his course. Before Mash or his father could react, the man fell to the ground. The monsternite advanced toward the tree, ignoring Mash and the two men. The monsternite thrust his head into the storage pouch, ripped it from the branch and threw it to the ground. Mash's family's belongings now lay across the field.

His father rushed to protect his mother. He scaled the tree before the monsternite could destroy the pouch she was in, too. "Get out of there!"

Mash watched from his position in the sky as time seemed to slow. The monsternite's enormous head swung in the direction of his pouch next.

"Beverly!" Mash howled.

He dove beneath the beast and aimed a knife at the monsternite's belly. He threw the knife as hard as he could until half the blade sunk into the monster's body. Another roar emerged from the beast, and a tail flew in Mash's direction. The tail slammed Mash against the tree's trunk and held him there. Mash struggled, but the monster didn't hold him there for long. Mash fell to the ground.

The beast, now with both feet planted on the ground, faced Mash once more. Mash pressed himself against the tree, but there was no-where to run. The monsternite let out one last roar, his breath smelling of rotting fish, and then crashed his tail into the trunk right above Mash's head and then flew away. Mash clapped his hands over his ears and squeezed his eyes shut as his ears pounded painfully.

Mash's father said something, but it was garbled and sounded like they were underwater. Mash rubbed his ears but kept his eyes shut. His father touched his shoulder, and Mash opened one of his eyes. "Are you alright?" Mash's father spoke slower and louder the second time, annunciating each syllable.

Mash moved his head side to side and squinted again. He was alive. Mash's father helped him to his feet and gestured over his shoulder in the direction the man had fallen from the monsternite. Mash followed his father to the spot while his mother stayed behind to try to clean up some of the damage. When they were close enough to see the man, Mash averted his eyes in disgust. The man had been thrown against the tree before he fell to the ground, and a sharp branch was lodged below his ribs. Mash collapsed to his knees and dry heaved.

When he regained his composure and a bit of his hearing, he asked, "Do you know who he is, Father?"

"I do not. He looks to be someone who works for the King and Queen." While Mash and his father wore a shirt and shorts woven out of grass and leaves, this man wore a tunic made of linen that was dyed blue. It was similar to the one Bushraal wore when they first met. Mash's father touched the hilt of a dagger attached to the man's leather belt. The decorative dagger handle bore an etched image of a royal crest—a merman and mermaid with long hair that they seemed to share and two tails with the fins crossed on top of one another. "But that doesn't explain why he was riding a monsternite. I didn't think the mermaids and the monsternites were allies."

"They're not." Mash coughed and covered his mouth before anything came up. "Nautica would've mentioned that."

"I need you to help me dig, Mash. You don't have to touch the body, but we need to bury it. We cannot just leave him here."

Mash rubbed his ringing ears again. "Why do we have to do anything for him? He was trying to kill us."

"Monsternites don't like people, Mash. If it wanted to kill you, it would've. It was looking for something"

"Beverly." Mash tried to run to the tree, but his shaky knees brought him back to the ground. He touched the back of his head and saw more blood on his fingers. His eyes rolled back into his head, and Mash passed out.

CHAPTER NINE

A large rip in the side of Mash's parents' sleeping pouch let light from the rising sun stream in. His mother sat beside him. Mash sat up and grabbed his head in pain. "Where's Beverly?"

She reached for his shoulders to encourage him to lie back down. "The visitor is asleep in your pouch."

"You know?" Mash held his breath and searched his mother's stony expression.

"Your father told me after the attack. I want her out of our home."

Mash sat up again. "I never meant to bring her here. I'm sorry. All I have to do is get her to the castle—"

She held up her hand. "All you have to do? You have never been to the castle, Mash. Is that where you were all this time? On your way to the castle? Your father is going to bring the girl to Olivia. She will deal with it."

"Olivia is the one who said I could go! She was going to go with us, but she must've gotten caught up in something else."

"It is not the journey I am concerned about, Mash. I am not giving my blessing for my son to go searching for a portal to the Ama Ranth. Because I know what will happen. You will follow that girl right through."

Mash picked at a loose thread in the blanket.

"Am I right?" she pressed.

"I'm meant to be there, Mother. I know I am."

"You can make that decision when you are older, when I am not able to stop you. Then you can decide if you want to disappear and break your mother's heart."

Mash's own chest tightened at her words.

"What if I promise to come back?" he whispered.

His mother took his hands in hers. Her rough thumb moved back and forth between his hands. "You lied to me about the visitor. I want to trust you, but I do not know if I can."

"Mother, I have to do this. Beverly's counting on me. When I get her home safe, I'll come back." She shook her head, so he raised his voice a little. "It'll only take a few days if we can get to the castle fast enough. Then I'll stay here with you and dad until I'm old enough."

Her lip quivered, and a tear dropped down her cheek.

"Please don't cry."

"Just come back, Son. Please."

"I will. I promise."

She pulled him to her, squishing him into a tight hug that she didn't seem intent on releasing. Mash patted her back.

Mash's mother and Beverly didn't speak for the remainder of Beverly's time there. His mother begged him to stay until his father returned home from spreading the news of the monsternite attack in town, but Mash was in a hurry to begin their journey again. As his mother packed him a sack of food, he heard something splashing in the stream.

An aquasus stood with its duck feet in the water and bit a hunk of grass from the shoreline. It raised its head as Mash scurried down the tree.

Beverly followed him down the tree and rooted herself right next to it. She shook her head, making her golden hair swish. "No way."

"Come on, it's safe."

"That's what Bushraal said last time. There's no way I'm getting on one of those things again."

"Come on, Beverly. It could take days to get to the castle by foot."

Beverly leaned against the tree. "Hey, were there flowers on that hill last night?"

After the attack the night before, it had been a pile of packed dirt. But now dark purple blooms blanketed the mound where Mash's father had buried the man. They were so dark, they were almost black.

"Donch coilee." Mash shuddered.

"What does it mean?"

"It is the monsternites' color." His mother appeared next to Beverly at the base of the tree, and Beverly shuffled out of her way. "I did not figure it out until that first night you disappeared. Every time a monsternite flies by, more of the flowers turn donch coilee and shrivel up." She angled her back toward Beverly to face Mash. "Are you leaving now?"

"Yes, I think we must."

Mash's mother squeezed him into one last embrace and then ruffled his hair with a bit of a tug before she released it. "Remember your promise."

"Yes, Mother."

With her head down, Beverly thanked his mother and stood next to the aquasus. The aquasus flapped its wings, which made Beverly jump. Mash passed Beverly with a smirk in her direction and pet the aquasus. It knelt down to let him climb on its back. Mash swung his legs over behind the wings before the aquasus stood back up. He held his hand out to Beverly, who continued to act aloof.

"Come here. Feel the wings. They're oily like a duck's." He reached for her wrist and pulled her over, placing her hand against the white feathers of the outstretched wing. The aquasus ruffled its wing, and Beverly yanked her hand back. Trying again, she pet its feathers with two fingers, then stepped closer and stroked the feathers with her palm.

"It almost feels like our chickens at home," she said.

The aquasus blew air out through its nose and stomped its foot, which had become a hoof on dry ground. Beverly jumped back.

"She," said Mash.

"What?"

"It's a she. And you're going to have to try harder to be nice if she's going to allow you to ride her."

Petting the aquasus' muzzle this time, she said, "Sorry about that.

You are much prettier than a chicken. May I ride you?"

The aquasus bobbed its head, its shiny white hair flowing behind it. She bent her right front leg so that Beverly could hoist herself over her back. Mash patted the smooth white hair behind him, signaling for Beverly to get on. Beverly swung her leg over the aquasus' back just like Mash had.

"See? Not so scary," he said.

"We're not in the air yet."

"We will be soon. Are you ready?"

Beverly placed her hands on either side of his waist. "No."

The aquasus took a few steps as a running start and lifted off. The sudden movement made Beverly wrap her arms around Mash's waist and bury her head in his back. Mash inhaled the lilac-scented air as it brushed over his face.

"What's going on? I can't see anything! Is it raining?"

"We're just flying through a cloud." Mash reached his hand up to feel the wet, cool fog on his fingertips. They left the cloud behind, and the sun dried his damp skin. "Beverly."

"What?"

"Do you have your eyes closed?"

"Yes."

"Open them up. I promise we won't fall this time. You have to see this."

The sight had changed since last time they rode an aquasus. Along either side of the glistening river was the sprawling field of flowers. Instead of the purple splotches, like there had been in Mash's yard, there was a wavy line of purple following the direction of the river.

"Do you think that's from the monsternite that we saw last time or a different one?" asked Beverly.

"I don't know, but let's hope this isn't a regular route of theirs."

"Yeah, I hope not."

"At least we know we're going the right way. Do you see the castle in the distance?" Mash sat up straight and pointed to the horizon.

A purple stone castle sat at the base of a purple mountain range. The tops of the mountains were concealed in fog, so Mash couldn't tell for sure how big they really were. Four towers of varying heights reached toward the sky. Even though it was early afternoon, dark clouds hung over the castle. It looked like they were flying right into night, as if it were a place and not a time of day. The river flowed into a lake, which ended a half mile from the castle.

"I guess all of Flowerantha isn't connected by water," said Mash.

The aquasus descended, and Beverly squeezed Mash's waist to brace for impact. Her hooves hit the ground one by one, and she galloped to a stop. Mash dismounted and held his hands out to catch Beverly by the waist as she hopped down.

Beverly patted the aquasus' neck. "Thanks for not throwing me off like the last one did." The black eyes twinkled at her through fans of white eyelashes. The aquasus nodded and flew off back over the lake.

The castle loomed in front of them. It was so massive that it blocked out the sun, casting a shadow where Beverly and Mash walked. It was built on a rocky hill at the base of the mountain, and the castle's size rivaled the mountain next to it. Instead of a moat, it was surrounded by a desert to prevent individuals who traveled by water to get anywhere near the castle. Dry grass, blowing sand, and spiky shrubs and trees replaced what used to be a lake.

Mash held out his hand and squeezed Beverly's. "Are you ready for this?"

CHAPTER TEN

"Do you think May Lynn and Bushraal are here yet?" asked Beverly.

"They must be by now."

"How will we find them?"

"I think we need to find something like a waterfall. That's how you got to Flowerantha."

"You've never been in this castle? It's huge. How are we going to find anything?"

"Good question."

A voice from above boomed. "What are you children doing here?" A land walker guard holding a long spear shouted down at them from one of the watchtowers. Mash opened his mouth to say something, but the guard continued. "You should be inside. There is work to be done."

Beverly glanced at Mash, but his gaze remained up toward the guard. "Of course. We were just getting some fresh air." Beverly grabbed his wrist, but he ignored her.

"No excuses. Get inside!"

Mash stepped forward, and Beverly released his wrist and held his sleeve by the elbow instead. Her legs trembled as they advanced toward the doorway, which was too small for a monsternite to pass through. Beyond the door was a courtyard. In the center was a statue of a man jutting out from a sand dune piled up to the statue's knees.

Beverly tugged Mash's sleeve and cupped her hand up by her mouth. "Who is the statue of?"

Mash leaned in close to her ear. "The man is Shrewtonite."

A man ran up beside them and spoke in Floweranthan. Mash replied in Floweranthan to avoid arousing suspicion, and Beverly crossed her arms and nodded, pretending to know what was going on. The man gestured for Mash to follow him, and Mash said something else, pointing his thumb at Beverly. In response, the man shook his head and walked away, urging Mash to follow him.

Before following, Mash planted his hands on Beverly's shoulders. "Find someplace to hide. I will come find you in a little bit. This man thinks we work here, and he wants me to go help him move something."

Beverly panicked. "How will you find me?"

Mash took her hands and held them with the palms up. "I wish for two looking glasses, one for Beverly so that she can see where I am, and one for me so that I can see where she is." A small mirror appeared in each of Beverly's hands. Mash took one out of her hand and held it up to his eye and then buried it between the leaves in his shorts where a pocket would be. Beverly held the glass up to her eye like Mash did and gasped as she saw her own face. "It'll show you what I'm seeing," he said.

"Wow, where'd you learn to do that?"

"I got the idea from Tumpske." He touched Beverly's shoulder and hurried off after the man, leaving Beverly alone in the courtyard.

Mash followed the man down a corridor, Mash's leather sandals and the man's bare feet slapping against the stone floor. The man was tan and bald, and a scar sliced right through his eyebrow and down to his cheek, making his left eye droop.

"Where are we going?" Mash asked in Floweranthan.

"Filling the fountains. What, have you been on brick duty or something? You look terrible."

"Yeah, brick duty. It is hard work." Mash wiped his forehead like he had just been working in the hot sun.

"I was on brick duty all last week. But they want us working on the fountains now for some reason. Those sand bags are even heavier than the bricks."

A tall, wiry young man with dirty brown hair that brushed his shoulders was already at the fountain, heaving a sandbag onto the edge of the fountain. He slashed the corner of the canvas bag with a knife, and the sand poured into the basin.

"Good, you are back," the young man said.

"I brought some help." The bald man gestured to Mash. "He came from brick duty."

"Oh, brick duty. I hear that is one of the worst jobs."

"It is pretty bad."

Mash snuck a peek at the circular piece of glass in his hand. Beverly appeared to be running through some sort of dining hall with long tables set up. "Where are you going, Beverly?" he whispered.

"What was that you said?" asked the older, bald man.

"Nothing." He shoved the glass back into his pocket. "What do we do here?"

The young man nodded toward a wheelbarrow overflowing with fifty-pound canvas bags of sand. "I just reloaded the wheelbarrow. Grab a bag and start pouring."

"How many fountains are we supposed to fill?"

"Five," said the young man. "Four inside at each of the corners of the castle and the one in the courtyard."

Mash heaved a sandbag out of the wheelbarrow and dropped it onto the ledge of the fountain. A puff of sand wafted into his face, and he sneezed. The young man offered him a knife, but he pulled out one of his throwing knives that he had wished for earlier. He poked the knife into the fabric, and dragged it to try to cut a hole. His other hand holding the top of the bag slipped, and the bag hit the floor with a bang. Sand poured out over his feet, and he rushed to pick the bag up again.

The young man laughed. "Good job."

"Come on, boys, hurry up. I do not want to miss the meal." The older man grabbed the other side of Mash's bag to help him lift it and ripped the top without using a knife. The two supported the bottom of the bag against the fountain while the rest of the sand drained out.

"I am Mash, by the way." Mash put his palm to his chest.

The younger man made the same gesture. "I am Lontano, but you can call me Lonny."

The older man nodded as he put his hand over his bare chest. "I am Dormir."

"Why are they making us fill these fountains anyway?" asked Mash.

Lonny stopped lifting the next sandbag and balanced the bag on its end in the wheelbarrow. "It is better not to ask questions. Why do you think my lips look like this?"

For the first time, Mash inspected Lonny's face. His irregularity wasn't as obvious as Dormir's scar until he brought attention to it. Lonny had large lips that sagged into a frown.

Lonny tugged on his bottom lip. "This is one of the monsternite's punishments for insubordination. The punishment for talking back was to stretch my lips."

Mash cringed and brought his fingers to his own lips. They were gritty and tasted like sand. "What other punishments are there?"

"You should see my brother's lips. His are even worse. They seem to like to do things to people's faces so that the punished can serve as an example," said Lonny. "It used to be little cuts, like a snipped nostril or earlobe, but lately, they have gotten into stretching. They like to experiment with different punishments."

Dormir touched his scar with his middle finger. "This is an experiment gone wrong. They were trying to put a device in my eye to prevent me from blinking. I was struggling, their tool slipped, and I ended up like this." His hand balled into a fist.

"Do the monsternites do all of this?"

"No, they employ the zomps to take care of it," said Lonny.

Mash grumbled. "I had my own zomp encounter just yesterday." The men went back to work transferring sandbags, so he changed the subject. "I heard there are visitors in Flowerantha. Do you think the sand in the fountains has anything to do with them?"

Dormir's eyes darted, and his scar twitched when he moved his forehead. "Are you crazy? Did you not understand Lonny's warning? Do not say things like that around here."

Footsteps echoed in the hall behind them, and Mash forgot about the sand dribbling out of the bag he was holding against the fountain.

"Who is coming now?" asked Dormir gruffly.

Mash fumbled with his bag when he saw the two figures—a small girl with long dark hair and a taller boy with wavy blond hair and blue eyes that were unmistakable even in the dim hallway. Their clothes were pristine, and they stood out next to the three dusty males loading sand.

"Did you find Beverly?" Mash asked Bushraal in Floweranthan.

Bushraal leaned closer to Mash and said in a low and threatening voice, "No, I thought she was with you. If you let anything happen to her..."

May Lynn kept quiet, but her head swished from side to side as she tried to locate her friend.

"What is he doing here? Is he supposed to be some kind of soldier?" Lonny nodded his head in Bushraal's direction.

Mash's eyebrows shot up. "You know English?"

"Yes, most of the land walker guards here do not, so we use it to communicate when we do not want them to understand."

"Well, we understand it." May Lynn stepped forward, her soft-spoken voice sounding more authoritative like Olivia's with only a slight waver.

Bushraal puffed out his chest. "Indeed, yes, we do. I have some unfinished business with this russet, and I insist he come with me. You can handle the rest of the task on your own?"

Lonny put his hands on his hips. "No we cannot. Not really. We have many more bags to go."

"Get back to work," Dormir said in his gravelly voice, like he had been inhaling sand for days. He threw an empty bag at Lonny.

May Lynn took another step forward, standing between Bushraal and the men. She commanded, "Stop goofing off, or you'll all be in trouble!"

At her harsh tone, the workers bowed their heads. "Yes, miss. Take him."

"Graciyoo." She took Bushraal's arm, and Mash followed, his jaw slack. Bushraal flashed her an appreciative look.

"You would fit in nicely here," Bushraal said, putting his hand over hers.

"Where did that come from?" whispered Mash, trailing behind them.

"Beverly's mom." Her lips curled into a demure smile. "With five kids, there's a lot of yelling in that house sometimes." Her smile disappeared a second later. "Is Beverly okay?"

"Yes, she is. We had to split up so no one got suspicious." Mash reached into his pocket and pulled out the looking glass. "This shows me what she sees." He held it in both hands and studied it. She was running through a hallway much like the one in which they were standing. "All these hallways look the same."

"Where did you go after your fell from the aquasus?" asked Bushraal. "After I fought off the monsternite, we landed and tried to find you."

"We met a zomp who zapped us all the way back to my home."

"Was that Tumpske?" asked May Lynn.

"Yes, how did you know?"

"We met him, too." Bushraal frowned. "He told us that you were halfway to the castle and that we should hurry up."

"That doesn't make any sense," said Mash.

The hallway opened up into a circular entryway. On the left were doors that led to a large dining room. To the right were two other hallways. Tired workers with dirty faces and hands and disheveled clothes trudged out of each of the corridors and into the open double doors of the dining room.

"This must be the meal Lonny and Dormir were talking about," said Mash.

May Lynn stood on the tips of her toes. "Do you think Beverly is in this crowd?"

Mash took the looking glass back out of his pocket. The glass showed the back of someone wearing a shirt made of twigs. Shoulders of other people came in to view around the edges. "I think so, yes."

The three pressed their backs against the nearest wall to watch the sea of people with their solemn faces drift by.

May Lynn spotted Beverly first. "There you are!"

Beverly pushed past a couple workers with blank expressions and ran to May Lynn, collapsing against her in a hug. May Lynn squeezed her back, and the girls jumped up and down a little. Then Beverly reached for Bushraal but stopped.

"Good to see you, too," said Mash.

"Oh stop, I'm happy I found you. I broke my mirror like ten minutes after you left." Beverly presented a shard of glass that was one-third the size of the original circular piece. "I could still kind of see, but I still didn't know where I was going because all—"

"These hallways look the same," Mash and Beverly said in unison.

Mash held up his own looking glass. "That explains all the running around in the wrong direction I was seeing."

"We were so worried about you," said May Lynn. "I'm glad you made it to the castle."

"Now I can figure out how to return you both home," said Bushraal. He clasped May Lynn's hand and squeezed it.

Mash gathered them into a huddle while the last of the crowd brushed past them. "I think the fountains are the key. There are five, and I think one must lead to the Ama Ranth."

"Well, we should go while everyone's eating dinner," said May Lynn.

"Good idea." Bushraal patted her on the shoulder. "We should split up so we can move quickly and cover more ground."

May Lynn squirmed. "I don't know if that's a good idea."

"We are not splitting up again," said Mash.

Bushraal bared his teeth at Mash. "I am not risking it. We need to move quickly."

Mash broke the huddle and stood nose to nose with Bushraal. "And we can do that all together."

"Fine, I will go alone," said Bushraal.

Beverly grabbed his arm. "Bushraal, don't go."

"May Lynn, you think we should stay together, right?" asked Mash.

May Lynn was caught off guard by his question. She stared at her hands. "I see Mash's point, but if Bushraal thinks we don't have time, then I trust him."

Bushraal's face softened. "Thank you. Now, Beverly, who are you going with?"

Beverly crossed her arms. "I'm staying with Mash, and you should, too."

May Lynn frowned. "Beverly. You're being impossible."

Beverly pouted. "I am not being impossible. I just don't want to get separated again. I fell off a *flying horse*, May Lynn. And I didn't know if you got eaten by a *dinosaur*. I just want to know you're safe."

"Beverly." Bushraal tried a soothing tone instead of a stern one. "I understand that you're afraid. Getting you home is my job, and I am not going to fail."

"Fine, you go, but May Lynn should stay here," said Beverly.

Bushraal smoothed down his vest. "May Lynn, are you coming?" He outstretched his hand to her. Her eyes darted from Bushraal to Beverly's squinted eyes and set jaw, then back to Bushraal.

She sighed. "Bushraal, it's not worth the risk for me. I'm sorry. We already lost Beverly once."

His hand dropped to his side. "Very well." He spun on his heel.

"Bushraal, wait." Mash handed Bushraal his looking glass. "Take this. We'll use Beverly's broken one. At least you'll know where we are."

Bushraal snatched the glass, and with one last glance at May Lynn, he was gone.

May Lynn's gaze did not leave his back, and Beverly stood behind her and held her shoulders. "You made the right decision."

"I hope so. Do you think he'll forgive me?"

Mash piped up. "Bushraal doesn't seem to be the forgiving type." Beverly shot him a death stare. "But it's you, so yes. I think so."

CHAPTER ELEVEN

"We need a plan," said Mash. "And we can't look too suspicious. If any guards spot us, we might have to get punishment like Lonny had."

"Is that what happened to Lonny?" asked May Lynn. "I thought something looked a little strange, but I didn't want to say anything."

"Yeah, their lips were stretched for talking back."

May Lynn shivered.

"So what's the plan?" asked Beverly. "Which fountain do you think is the right one?"

Mash scratched his head. "We'll have to dig them out and try them all, I guess."

May Lynn stared at the floor. "I can't go without saying goodbye to Bushraal."

Beverly sighed. "I don't want to either. Let's just figure out what fountain it is, and then try to find Bushraal. Deal?"

May Lynn still didn't raise her eyes. "Sure."

"Let's start with one inside the castle that I didn't fill," said Mash.

"I saw one of them when I was walking around the castle before," said Beverly. "Hopefully I can find it again."

The three jogged down one of the long hallways. Mash halted and put both his arms out to stop them. May Lynn froze just short of his arm, but Beverly wasn't paying attention and plowed into him. He grabbed her and put his hand up to his lips. "I hear something." He swung his head around in search of an escape route. Letting go of Beverly, he grabbed the iron handle of the nearest wooden door and flung it open. He held the door and motioned for the girls to go in.

The crack beneath the door provided a sliver of light. Otherwise, the room was cloaked in darkness. Mash closed the door behind them just as a sound like thunder passed the door. The three of them huddled near the door, and as the sound got quieter, Mash reached his hand out to the door handle. The thundering sound returned, even louder than before. The floor beneath them trembled.

"Is this an earthquake?" whispered Beverly. Mash put his finger up to his mouth again while May Lynn made a frantic cutting motion across her throat. •

The three of them were thrown back when the door burst open from some outside force. Despite how large the doorway was, it was still too small for the enormous monsternite to fit through. The beast stuck its head in first and roared as Mash and the girls crab-walked as fast as they could to the back wall. The extra light illuminated the rest of the room.

On the left side was a table with straps on it. Tools that appeared to be doctor's instruments lined shelves on the wall above the table. A metal bookshelf stood against the wall by the door. It held different sized metal balls on each of the shelves. The beast swung its great head, slamming it into the shelves. The sides of the structure bent upon impact, but it did not tip over. The back of it was secured to the wall. While the beast slammed its snout repeatedly, bending the metal more and more, Mash scanned the room. On the right wall was a pile of the same poles that made up the shelf that the metal balls were resting on. Mash snatched one of the poles and tossed one to Beverly. She reacted and caught it in midair.

"Nice catch," said Mash. "Remember our weapons lesson?" Beverly nodded. "Time to put it into practice."

Mash ran at the monsternite and drove the pole into the gums of his bared teeth. The monsternite swung his head, but Mash dodged it, and the beast knocked its skull into the shelf again. The metal scaffolding groaned and collapsed into itself, and the solid balls crashed to the floor one by one and rolled right in Beverly and May Lynn's direction.

May Lynn shielded herself, but Beverly faced the rolling balls head on. Beverly's foot intercepted one that was coming right at May Lynn's ankles and she yelped. May Lynn cracked an eye open and dodged the next ball that came her way. Learning from her mistake, Beverly used the pole to block the balls coming toward her. Mash tried to back up to the girls, but one ball clipped his heel, and he fell to the ground. Beverly shuffled over to him and dropped her knees to the ground with her legs pointed outward to deflect the last ball that was headed right for Mash.

"Where'd you learn to do that?" he asked.

"Soccer practice!"

"Dodgeball in gym class is really paying off, too," May Lynn said as she jumped out of the way.

"Yeah, dodgeball was a lot smarter idea." Beverly massaged her shins.

Mash heaved the pole again and swatted the monsternite on the nose. The beast roared and backed out of the room. Mash stuck his head out. "He's still out there."

"How are we going to get out?" asked May Lynn.

"Yeah, what if he never leaves? What if we starve here?"

"That's not likely, but just in case, we'll have to think of a reason for him to leave," said Mash. "Beverly, do you still have the knife I gave you?"

Beverly's hand went to the spot on her dress where the knife was tied. "Yes, it's still there." She worked to untie the leather knot at her side and held the knife out to Mash.

He shook his head. "You can do it. Remember what we practiced?"

"Well, yeah, but—"

"Just try."

She stood in the doorway and squared herself off to the monsternite. Hesitating, she looked at Mash for some reassurance. He nodded and motioned for her to go on. Taking a deep breath, she whipped the knife out the door, and the monsternite bellowed as it nicked his neck.

"I did it!" She flung her arm around Mash's shoulder, and he squeezed her back.

"Great job, but I think we need to aim for something more sensitive, like its eyes," said Mash. "Its skin is too tough. Do we have anything else to throw?"

Beverly left her position and hurried to the wall with all the medical tools on it. "May Lynn, come here and help me carry this stuff."

May Lynn helped Beverly collect the instruments. They carried hammers and wrenches, a saw, some knives, a crude-looking screwdriver, and anything that would fit in their arms.

Mash picked up a knife in one hand and a screwdriver in the other. He closed one eye to aim, and let the knife fly first. It missed its target and zipped by the monsternite's massive head. He readjusted his stance and pointed the screwdriver at the moving target. The screwdriver seemed to glide in slow motion when he released it. It plunged right under the beast's eyelid into the yellow pupil. The monsternite tossed its head and howled like an injured dog.

Beverly hid her face behind her hands. "Gross! I almost feel sorry for him."

The monsternite bucked its head but did not cease its pacing in front of the doorway.

"Maybe we can trip him somehow," said Mash.

Beverly eyed the scattered metal balls. "Bowling anyone?"

"That might work," said May Lynn.

"What's bowling?"

"Oh, you'd love it. You just roll a ball at a bunch of pins and try to knock them all down. I'm not great at it, but it's pretty fun. May Lynn's better than I am." Beverly picked up one of the balls. "Normally there are holes to put your fingers in, but we can just palm it. That's what my older brothers do."

"Sure, whatever you say," said Mash.

"May Lynn, show him how it's done." Beverly handed her the ball.

May Lynn rolled her eyes. Leaning her top half out the door, she swung her right arm back like a pendulum and released the ball. It careened down the hall to where the monsternite had just come back around to pace the other way, and the ball hit its tail.

"Direct hit!" Beverly shouted, holding up her hand for a high five.

May Lynn returned the high five without much vigor. "Yeah, but it didn't do anything. I don't think this bowling thing was such a good idea."

"It's just the first one. I'm hoping he'll either get really annoyed or trip on one of them," said Beverly. "Mash, you want to go next?"

"Uh, why don't you go so that I know more of what I'm supposed to be doing?"

"Chuck the ball at the monsternite, Mash. There's really nothing to know," said Beverly with a playful jab of her elbow.

"Yes, but if we're making sport of it, I want to be sure I know the rules," he said.

"Okay, fine, I'll go next." Beverly picked up another one of the balls and balanced it on her right hand in front of her face. It tee-tered, but she recovered and steadied it with her left hand. Beverly steadied herself, took three steps, and released the ball. It veered to the right, bounced off a wall, and managed to come to rest beside the monsternite's left foot. "That was a warm up." She lifted another ball into position. Before Mash or May Lynn could object, she took her approach again and released. The ball went straighter this time, but as a result, it rolled right through the monsternite's legs.

"Goal," deadpanned May Lynn.

"Alright, let me try this." Mash picked up a ball, bounced it in his hands, and practiced his approach without letting go. He did this several times until he found a ball he liked.

"If you ever make it to our home, or the Ama Ranth, be sure to join a bowling team," said Beverly. "You look like a pro already and you haven't even thrown yet."

Mash stood near the door, took one step, and launched the ball into the air, more like a softball throw than bowling. The ball smacked into the monsternite's shin, and they got a reaction. The monsternite let out a short, bark-like roar of annoyance. He flashed his teeth through the door again, but then went back to pacing.

"It's not working," said May Lynn in despair.

One by one, the three of them picked up a ball and launched it into the hallway. As each ball made contact, the monsternite grunted and jerked its body away from the impact. Its great nostrils flared, and the gray feathers along its shoulders and back stood up on end like an angry cat's fur. The edge of the beast's foot made contact with one of the bigger balls, and it stumbled, its shoulder crashing against the wall opposite them.

"I like this bowling thing as a game, but it seems pretty ineffective." Mash searched for something else to use against the monsternite. "I have another plan." He grabbed a rolled up lasso of rope that was over the table with the straps on it. "If he stumbles again, I'm going to tie his feet together."

"He has wings, too, Mash," said May Lynn.

"I'll get those, too."

"How is that a good idea?" asked Beverly. "He has teeth, too!"

Mash ignored her last comment. "While I'm tying him up, you run. Find another room, or if you can make it to the fountain, do it."

Beverly tried to grab his arm to stop him. "Mash, no."

"Beverly." He faced her, stood right in front of her, and placed his hands on her shoulders like he had when they first arrived at the castle. "The only way out is through those fountains. And the only way to those fountains is through that monsternite. Please, let me do this for you and May Lynn. I will be fine."

Beverly's mouth was pinched in an expression of concern, but she managed a half smile. "This is a terrible idea, but if you think it'll work."

He squeezed her shoulders. "At least it's not bowling."

Beverly laughed and pushed his chest away. "May Lynn, you ready?"

"As ready as I'm going to be," she said.

The girls positioned themselves at the door, right behind Mash, who was armed with the looped rope. They waited for the monsternite to trip. It had to happen eventually. There were so many tools and metal balls scattered across the floor that there was no way the monsternite could avoid stepping on them forever. And he didn't. Whenever he hit one and sway to the side, Mash flinched and stepped into the hallway, and the girls crouched into a racing position. But the monster recovered, and the three returned to their vigilant positions.

"If this hurts half as much as stepping on a Lego, this is going to take him right to his scaly knees," said Beverly.

"I have no idea what that means, but I'd like to see that happen." Mash tightened the rope between his hands.

The monster planted his massive foot on one of the tools and let out a pitiful yelping roar. It stumbled a little, but once again was back on two solid feet.

Mash pumped his fists. "Come on, come on."

The monsternite paced again, this time with its back to the door. It treaded on a tool with a spiked ball on the end and howled. Off balance, it stepped on a second instrument and lunged forward without any leverage to catch himself. Its face hit the ground, and Mash didn't waste another second. He sprinted toward the beast and yelled to the girls to go. Beverly darted out first calling to May Lynn to follow.

Beverly sat on the edge of the leathery leg and swung her legs over. May Lynn followed and crawled over the ankle, leaning in the opposite direction to avoid the sharp yellowed claws on the foot that was almost as big as her. Once they had cleared the monsternite, they sped toward the end of the hall. The fountain was in sight. Beverly grabbed the side and used it to swing herself around to the back, and she and May Lynn crouched behind the stone fountain.

"If this doesn't work, we're trapped again." Beverly peeked over the edge of the fountain.

"I thought of that," said May Lynn.

They waited for a few minutes, but there was only a loud moaning noise and then silence. Then, there was a loud roar.

Beverly flinched. "Do you think we should go back for him?"

"No!" May Lynn pulled her back down.

"Okay, fine."

They waited another minute before the sound of pounding footsteps met their ears.

"It's definitely not a monsternite," said Beverly, but she remained in her crouched position.

Mash came into view, ran right into the fountain, and used it to stop his momentum.

Beverly leapt up and was at his side. "Is it safe now?"

"Yes, we should be alright. I didn't realize how long that rope actually was. He'll probably break through it eventually, but he's tied up right now. The only thing I left were his teeny tiny useless hands."

"Great job!" Beverly held up her hand for a high five. Mash stared at it and grabbed it. "You're supposed to slap it." She held her hand up again, and this time he slapped it. "Very good."

Mash dug his hand into the overflowing well of sand. "This is not going to be easy. I don't have any wishes left." He stuck his other hand in and then threw the handful of sand to the floor.

May Lynn cupped a handful of sand but dropped it back into the well and wiped her hands off on her leafy skirt. "Is it just me, or is the sand moving?"

Beverly shrieked. The sand was indeed moving. A dozen creatures that were a combination of rats and insects, with rats' heads, scaly backs, insect feet, and long, rat-like tails skittered from the depths of the sand.

"Maoompy!" Beverly backed up against the wall. "I am not going anywhere near that."

The rat-insect creatures scurried over the edge of the fountain, onto the floor, and down the hallway.

"Where the heck are they going?" May Lynn stood on her tiptoes and pressed her back into the wall next to Beverly.

"I have no idea." Mash continued to dig, pushing the rat-insects out of the way. "Are you girls going to help?" May Lynn shook her head while Beverly stood against the wall, refusing to move. "This is going to take forever if I have to do it myself."

"When those things leave, then maybe," said Beverly. One of the critters reached the edge of the fountain and climbed over the stone lip, headed in Beverly's direction. She yelped and danced on her tiptoes out of the way behind May Lynn.

Mash dug a few more handfuls of rat-insect-filled sand out of the fountain before he stopped, brushing his hands off on his shorts. "This is hopeless. We have to figure out a different way."

"Um, guys," said May Lynn, "do you hear that?"

The three froze. Something rumbled down the hall.

"Is that the monsternite?" asked Beverly. They couldn't move. Even if they could, there was nowhere to go. They were trapped at a dead end with no escape. The rumbling sound grew closer as if a violent thunderstorm was driving right toward them. A sudden crash of the thunder caused them all to jump. The sound stopped, and they exchanged nervous glances. After a second, running footsteps that sounded like leather slapping against the stone floor replaced the thundering. A mop of wavy dark blond hair came into view.

May Lynn grinned, and even Mash sighed in relief. "Was that you finishing off the monsternite?" asked Mash.

Panting, Bushraal said, "I thought you might need some help."

CHAPTER TWELVE

Mash grabbed Bushraal's forearm and brought him in for a hug, taking Bushraal by surprise. "Thanks for taking care of it for us."

Bushraal backed away and tried to fight a smile, but his lips betrayed him. "You did pretty well yourself. That monsternite looked quite banged up before I got to him. Its wings were still tied together."

Mash chuckled and slapped Bushraal on the back. "I guess I did alright!"

"Yes, you did. And you were right. We should stick together."

"I'm so glad you're back." May Lynn gazed at him in admiration.

"I had to finish what I started. I wanted to. What is the plan?" They filled him in on the progress of searching the fountains. "You will be happy to know that I still have all three of my wishes." Mash, Beverly, and May Lynn jumped and cheered. "I wish that the sand..."

"And bugs," said Beverly.

"And bugs would disappear from this fountain."

At Bushraal's word, the sand and rat-insects vanished with a pop. Then, the tub of the fountain filled again, and water spilled down from the top tier to the middle and splashed into the basin.

"So, how do we do this?" asked Beverly.

"I'll try." Mash stepped over the edge of the fountain and into the water. Letting the water from the top tier fall over his head, he closed his eyes. The other three waited.

"Perhaps it will not work for you," said Bushraal.

Mash opened one of his eyes. "What do you mean?"

"No one from Flowerantha has ever gone to the Ama Ranth."

Mash lifted a finger. "That we know of."

Bushraal shook his head. "Let Beverly try."

Mash put out his hand, and Beverly took it, holding down her dress as she stepped into the basin with him.

"This is kind of cold," she said.

"Mash, get out." Bushraal pointed his thumb over his shoulder, and Mash climbed out and folded his arms. Nothing happened.

The water dripped onto Beverly's face, and she brushed her wet bangs aside. "I'm still here."

"This must not be the right one. Onto the next." Bushraal held out his hand and helped Beverly climb back out. She shivered.

The four of them took off back down the hall. They climbed over the deceased monsternite and came to a fork in the passageway. Beverly hesitated and then darted down the hallway on the right.

"Is this the right way?" asked Bushraal.

"I have no idea." But they kept running. She stopped. "No, this doesn't look familiar at all. Sorry! Sorry!"

The boys sighed, and they all spun on their heels and bolted back down the other path. At the end of the next hallway, there was still no fountain.

"I swear this is where it was." They looked doubtful. "I swear!"

"Wait, I think she's right," said May Lynn.

"Thank you, May Lynn."

"Look." May Lynn bent down and touched the floor. Mash and Bushraal knelt down next to her. On the floor was a bronze pipe surrounded by a circle a couple shades darker than the rest of the floor. The spot on the floor was damp to the touch.

Beverly shuffled her feet. "Sand, too."

Bushraal stood, balled up his fists, and slammed them against the wall.

"It has to be this one," said Mash. "Why else would they go

through the trouble of moving it? And where did it go?"

May Lynn snapped her fingers. "Bushraal, do you still have that mirror thing Mash gave you?" He stared at her without answering. "The looking glass thing that we used to know where you were."

"Yes, I think so." He patted the bamboo of his shorts and pulled out the small glass disc. He put it over his eye and saw his own face as they were seeing him.

"Could we use it to see where the fountain is? Like, re-wish it?"

"It's worth a try. I wish to see the location of the fountain that used to be located here." Bushraal held the glass up to his eye. "It is dark, wherever it is. I do not recognize the location."

"Can I see?" Bushraal surrendered the glass to Mash. "Wait. This cannot be it. I think I know where it is. You both should recognize this place."

Beverly took the glass next. "No way."

May Lynn held it up to her eye last. "Is that where I think it is?"

The room was dark, but dim streams of light revealed some telling details in the room. A metal structure that was dented stood doubled over on one side of the room. On one side of was a table with straps on it. The fountain butted right up against the table, pushing it against the wall so that the table stood on only two of its legs.

"Well, I'll give it to them. It is the last place we would think to look," said Mash.

"What is it?" asked Bushraal.

"It's the room we were just in when the monsternite was trying to get us," said Beverly.

"After you." Mash swept his arm in front of himself, and Beverly moved first. "On second thought," he said, blocking her path, "maybe I should lead. You got us lost last time you led."

Beverly gave him a shove.

꙰꙰꙰

Back down the previous hallway, they stopped when they neared the door in question. The fallen monsternite body had been removed, but now there was something else guarding the door.

"Tumpske, you rascal." Mash ground his fist into his other hand.

"We need to get into that room. And no tricks this time."

"Ah, cerulean, Mister Mash. Bevvy. Friends of Mister Mash and Bevvy." The creature nodded at each of them. His voice bounced like a ball and ricocheted off of the stone surrounding them.

Mash advanced toward Tumpske, towering over him. "Are you going to let us pass?"

Tumpske held up his three-fingered palm facing them. "Stay where you are."

Unabashed, Mash ran his finger along the doorframe. "What is this room used for anyway?"

"Punishment." Tumpske stuck his tongue out whenever he paused. "But I is a lousy tour guide, ya know, Mister Mash. I tried to keep you away from the castle. But you found her. Get back where you came from, won't ya."

"If that's the punishment room, what were those metal balls used for?" asked Beverly.

"Stretching the body parts." Tumpske's giant eyes did not blink as he waited for a reaction from them. Beverly gulped and put her fist over her lips, and May Lynn shuddered.

"Tumpske, I don't want to have to do this to you." Mash made eye contact with Bushraal, and they both reacted at the same time. They lunged at Tumpske, but before they reached him, Tumpske flicked his wrist and sent the boys flying back toward the wall. They slammed their backs and fell to the hard floor in a heap.

Tumpske clasped his tiny hands together. "You leaving this place yet?"

Bushraal growled. "Not a chance. I wish for two swords."

"Four," said Mash. "The girls are plenty capable of defending themselves, too."

Bushraal eyed May Lynn as a sword materialized in each of his hands. He tossed the second sword to Mash. "Exactly as I taught you now."

"I don't need a weapon." With his hands still clasped, Tumpske's feet left the ground, and he hovered in the air just above Mash's and Bushraal's heads. "Scorso, the monsternite in charge, he give me protection from being hunted if I keep everyone away from this here fountain. Ya see, Mister Mash, we are a delicacy to the monsternites.

But we be more valuable living than dead. Not the case for you, my friends. At least, not the boys. The visitor girls, though..." Tumpske held his hand out toward May Lynn and Beverly.

"You will not touch them!" Bushraal swung his sword at Tumpske's throat. The sword turned to sand, and it poured down over Bushraal's still clenched fists. Beverly grabbed a handful of the berries on May Lynn's back and pulled her closer to the wall behind them.

Tumpske sank back down to the ground. "I make a deal. Visitor girls for whatever you wants."

"No deal," said Bushraal. He shook the sand from his hands and put his fists up instead.

"Bribery and favors be the only way to get by me now."

Mash's sword was still drawn, and his muscles were flexed and ready to fight, but he didn't move.

"What else do you want?" asked Bushraal.

Mash's cool gray eyes were wild. "Are you really going to bargain with him? He just tried to barter with Beverly and May Lynn. He's a trickster. He's fooled me once. I don't want to have anything to do with him."

"I surprised you twos be working together." Tumpske drummed his tiny green fingers against each other, but the boys didn't react. "You don't know?" Tumpske's stuck-out tongue taunted them as they frowned back at him. Tumpske gestured to Bushraal. "Well, well. You a baby soldier, yeah?" He didn't wait for Bushraal to respond. "Your uncle, your father's brother, we on the same team, don't cha know. He was working for the monsternites, too."

"No! That cannot be true." Bushraal sprung at him at the same time as Mash did. Mash raised his right arm to attack from above, but the hilt struck Bushraal hard on the chin. Bushraal reeled and stumbled backward, losing his balance. Tumpske didn't flinch as Bushraal fell to the floor with a howl of pain.

"I not done," said Tumpske.

Mash dragged the sword across the floor in one hand while he reached for Bushraal with the other. Bushraal smacked his hand away and cradled his chin.

"Your uncle's working for Scorso, just like I am. He was on a mission to the home of Mister Mash here." He swung his hand in Mash's direction. Mash paled, and his jaw went slack.

"Ah, Mister Mash. You wanna tell him?"

Mash was shaking. He dropped the sword, and it clattered against the stone floor. "Bushraal, I didn't know."

Bushraal tore his eyes away from Tumpske to look at Mash. His eyebrows knitted in anger and confusion. His chin already bore a dark purple bruise.

"Go ahead, Mister Mash."

Mash was silent, his face frozen in horror.

"Fine, fine. I tell him. Your friend, Mister Mash here, he was 'sponsible for the death of your uncle."

Bushraal stared at Tumpske for a second, letting the news wash over him. He then gritted his teeth and turned on Mash. Bushraal leapt off the floor and slammed into Mash, causing Mash to tumble to the floor in a heap. Bushraal stood over him, and Tumpske watched in silence with his tongue sticking out. Tumpske let Bushraal land one punch right to Mash's temple while the girls shouted at him to stop before Tumpske waved his hand again and tossed Bushraal off of Mash.

"Like I say, neither of you is valuable alive. I would've made a deal with you, but since you won't give me what I be wanting, I gotta make sure you don't try and get to this fountain. And give you a taste of what will happen to you if you try again. Good luck getting home, girls." With that, Tumpske circled his hand in front of his body, and the boys were thrown into the punishment room. Mash's knee met the hard stone fountain, and he yelped in pain. The door slammed behind them, and a lock latched. The screams of Beverly and May Lynn sounded muffled and further away than just beyond the door.

Without touching him, Tumpske flung Bushraal to the wall with the broken shelf, and a chain wrapped itself around his body to secure him against the structure.

"Mister Mash, I's sorry for dis." Tumpske wrung his hands out and pointed to the table. Mash flew like a rag doll onto the leaning table. In moments, Mash's arms were tied down with scratchy rope that hurt his skin, and beads of sweat formed on his forehead.

"Beverly, get Nautica," he whispered to no one.

A bright light shone in his eyes, but he couldn't tell what the source of the light was. He could just make out the silhouette of Tumpske. His small hands held some kind of tool. Tumpske clamped the metal tool onto Mash's earlobe, and Mash's whole body jumped at the pressure. With his stubby fingers on Mash's forehead, Tumpske held Mash's head still. Tumpske reached across the table and grabbed a handful of small metal balls. The metal clinked together each time Tumpske took one of the balls out of his hand, and Mash felt more weight pulling down on his earlobe. He tried to move his hands to relieve the pressure on his ear, but the rope dug welts into his arm. Tumpske added ball after ball onto the end of the tool as tears sprung to Mash's eyes.

When he couldn't take it anymore, he cried out, "Stop, you're going to rip my ear off!"

Tumpske grunted. He retrieved a piece of fabric from his jacket pocket, wadded it up, and shoved it in Mash's mouth. The fabric tasted salty like sweat, but Mash tried to convince himself it was sea water as he gagged. Tears stung his eyes and left a wet trail down the sides of his face. Tumpske disappeared from view, and Mash was left with the bright light blinding him once again. He twisted his head to see where Tumpske went, but it only made his ear hurt even more. He squeezed his eyes shut and sobbed, waiting for it to end.

Maybe ten minutes or maybe an hour later—Mash couldn't be sure—Tumpske appeared again, blocking the light. He unbound the ropes, released the weights from Mash's earlobe, and flicked his wrist.

Mash flew across the room and collapsed. Chains formed around him where the ropes were and shackled him in place. He sagged against the nearest wall, cupping his trembling hand against his ear. Tumpske replaced him with Bushraal on the punishment table. Straining against his chain restraints, Mash touched his left ear, the lobe of which was now slightly longer than the right one. He closed his eyes when Bushraal grunted. Bushraal refused to cry out like Mash had. Mash pressed the heels of his hands over his ears. The door to the room burst open and slammed against the metal shelf that Mash was attached to, which jammed the bent metal into his shoulder blade.

"Time to go to the mountain," said a man's voice.

CHAPTER THIRTEEN

Mash opened his eyes to find himself in a small, square room that had a stone staircase leading up to the door. Unlike the smooth bricks in the castle, these walls were bumpy, like the cave he had slept in days earlier. He touched the tender spot on the side of his head where Bushraal had slugged him. He stood, staggered up the steps, and tried the door. "Locked. Of course. Nautica, if you can hear me, send help." There was only a dim light in his cell, so he could not tell what time of day it was. His stomach rumbled.

"I wish for a loaf of bread." He held out his hand, but only a puff of smoke appeared. He tried again anyway. "I wish for the key to this room." A smaller, more pitiful puff of smoke appeared in his hand this time. He walked back down the stairs and slumped on the floor.

He surveyed the damage to his body. His knee was covered in dried blood, but besides that minor injury and his stretched earlobe, he didn't seem to have any broken bones. He found a small pile of stones on the floor and threw them against the wall one by one to pass the time. He was surprised when he heard a similar sound come from the other side of the wall. "Bushraal?"

"You are lucky there is wall between us, russet," came Bushraal's muffled reply.

"Bushraal, we were going after the monsternite, not your uncle. I'm sorry he's gone. Truly. But he did destroy my home."

"I do not want to hear it." Mash could hear the fury in his voice. There was a faint bang on the wall, and Bushraal swore in Floweranthan. "*Gaff!*"

"What was that?"

"It was me punching your face."

Mash suppressed a laugh in spite of himself.

"If we get out of here alive, we are done. You stay out of my sight, or I will kill you."

"Bushraal—"

"Do not speak to me again unless you have a plan."

"What if you come up with a plan?"

"Just hope you come up with one first."

Mash picked up all the stones in one fistful and threw them on the opposite wall instead, harder this time. It was the second time in his life he felt this trapped. But this was unlike the safe haven of the waterfall cave where he had spent a night before this all began. He lay down on his side and cradled his stomach, which had rumbled again. He tried to sleep, but his mind was racing. He kept picturing Bushraal on the back of the monsternite the day his home was attacked. In one scenario, Mash pushed Bushraal off of the monsternite himself. In another scenario, Bushraal helped Mash and his father, and the monsternite never destroyed the house at all. And in yet another scenario, the two of them were strangers, just as Bushraal's uncle and Mash had been. The same exact thing happened—Bushraal was thrown from the monsternite, crashed into the roof, and landed dead on the ground. When Mash pictured Bushraal on the ground instead of his uncle, he became nauseated. Shivering with hunger and weakness, he drifted to sleep.

He woke with a start when the door to his cell creaked open and slammed back shut before he could react. A plate of food sat on the floor just inside his room. Mash crawled to the plate on his hands and knees. He picked up the bread, which was hard and stale, but he ate it anyway. The yellow cheese was discolored darker on one side. Mash tore it off and ate the good part. Still hungry, he ate the hard, darker-colored part, too. With a little more strength now, he paced the room. He inspected every crevice for a way out. He couldn't sit still any longer without trying to escape. Mash patted his shorts pocket. The knife he had wished for the previous day was gone. Whether it had disappeared or someone had taken it, he didn't know. Picking up one of the bigger rocks, which was shaped like a lopsided arrowhead, Mash jammed the rock in every crack around the door, trying to jimmy it open. It wasn't working, but it gave him something to do.

Without much nourishment in hours, Mash grew tired again. He leaned his back against the wall that divided his cell and Bushraal's and sank down, drawing his knees up to his chest. He heard a rhythmic sound coming from the other side of the wall. *Slap, slap, slap*, pause. *Slap, slap, slap*, pause. It sounded like Bushraal was pacing as his sandals hit the floor. His eyes drooped as he struggled to hold them open.

On what he assumed to be the second day of his captivity, the door cracked open again only long enough for someone to shove a cup in and close the door again. Some of the water sloshed out, and Mash staggered to the door to retrieve his drink. He licked his cracked lips and slung the water into the back of his throat. It wasn't very much, and it tasted like metal, but it was the most satisfying thing that had passed his lips in a while.

Mash lay on his back with outstretched limbs and stared at the ceiling. In the hopes that someone who could help would hear him, he sang all of the songs he knew in a loud, out-of-pitch tone. The second song in, Bushraal pounded at the wall next door, and Mash was glad for the company. The third song in, Mash began replacing the words of the chorus of a common Floweranthan folk song to suit his current situation:

We are all united
Our water is our life
Land and sea together
Can overcome all strife

We are all going to die here
Our water tastes like lye

Mash and Bush together
Die, die, die, die, die

At the fourth song, his mouth became parched again, and his fervent shouting diminished into plaintive whining. His lip trembled, and he bit it hard. "Someone will come," he whispered. "Knock it off, Mash. Someone will come." He didn't bother getting up when the door rattled again. Instead, he continued staring at the rock pattern on the ceiling that resembled crumpled paper.

Mash heard a voice coming from behind the door. "Mash! Bushraal! Are you in there?"

"Beverly?" His voice cracked.

"Mash, are you okay?"

"Beverly, is that you?"

"Yes, it's me."

"Mash, we only have one wish," said a woman's deep voice. Olivia was there, too. "We are going to get you out."

Mash wanted to rise, but his muscles felt heavy. He pushed himself up to a sitting position with much effort, his eyes locked on the door.

The lock clicked, and the door creaked open. Mash recognized a look of pity on Beverly's face when she saw him. His dark brown hair was matted and messy, his face was streaked with dirt, and what was left of his clothing was tattered into leafy rags. The place where Bushraal had slugged him had changed from an angry purple to a less harsh blue and yellow as it healed. Beverly barreled down the stairs two at a time and knelt beside him. She lay a hand gently on his forearm. Olivia followed, and May Lynn trailed behind. Olivia swung one of Mash's arms over her shoulder, and Beverly took the other arm.

Mash croaked through dry, thin lips. "Olivia, you have wings." White-feathered wings, just like an aquasus', protruded from Olivia's shoulder blades and reached down to the back of her knees.

"Yes, you will see why soon."

One slow step at a time, they were back in the dim hall.

"Bushraal's in there." Mash nodded at the door across from them.

"I figured as much," said Olivia. "We do not have any more wishes."

"I might." Mash took a deep breath as if the effort of speaking was taking every last ounce of energy he had. "My wishes were not working in that room. I stopped trying. If yours worked. Maybe mine will." He dropped his arm from Beverly's shoulders and held his hand out in front of him. "I wish for the key to this door." The key took form, but it was almost transparent. It took another couple seconds for it to become solid in Mash's hand.

Olivia reached for the key, but Mash said, "I'll do it. I owe him more than one." He maneuvered the key into the lock.

"Who is there?" Bushraal called from inside. Footsteps raced to the door. Mash pushed the door open, and Bushraal stood right inside, facing them. He looked a little better off than Mash, but barely. His chin was still a little bruised with a small scab where the sword's hilt had dug in. His bamboo vest was missing, and one of the sleeves on his blue shirt was ripped shorter than the other. He pushed back his dirty blond hair, and the group outside of the door noticed his bruised hand.

May Lynn grabbed it. "What happened?"

Bushraal squeezed her hand. Even with the dark circles under his eyes from lack of sleep, his blue eyes remained clear and piercing. "It was nothing." He scowled at Mash. "Let us get out of here so that I can get home and never see his face again."

They came to a ledge, where the hallway dropped off into the open mouth of a cave. The sound of battle raged below them. The soldiers shouted and monsternites roared, and metal clanged against rock and thudded against scaly flesh. The four monsternites occupied much of the space in the cave. Although there were a hundred soldiers, the monsternites overtook them with a swing of a tail or a stomp of a foot. The head monsternite, Scorso, was unmistakable with his inky black feathers while the other three monsternites' feathers were subdued grays and rusty reds. In the center of the cave stood a cylindrical glass structure filled with water. A golden-haired merman hovered in the water behind the glass.

Bushraal stood with his toes curled over the ledge. "What is going on? It looks like a war down there."

Olivia joined him at the ledge and watched the scene. "It is a rescue mission. That is why I could not join you on your quest. I was assembling the land walker army to rescue the king. He disappeared shortly after the visitors arrived, and we just found him in the cave, captured by the monsternites. As for rescuing you, I was in the right place at the right time when Beverly and May Lynn found me and asked for my help."

"How do we get down?" asked Bushraal. "Olivia, you cannot carry all of us."

"I will just have to take everyone down one at a time while my wings last," she said.

"Take us where?" asked Bushraal.

"Anywhere is better than that room," said Mash.

Olivia wrapped her arms securely around Beverly.

"Wait, why am I first?" Beverly tried to push Olivia's arms away, but Olivia only tightened her hold.

"You'll be okay, Beverly. I'll be right behind you," Mash said.

With Beverly secured, Olivia stepped off the landing and into the chaos.

"We need to get down there," said Bushraal.

"I can wait," said May Lynn.

"Yeah, Olivia will be right back," said Mash.

"No, we are both going now. I wish for wings." White wings with silver tips sprung out of the back of his shirt. The light reflecting off his wings coupled with his golden locks and angular jawline gave him an angelic appearance even with all the dirt and grime. He walked toward May Lynn with outstretched arms.

"You cannot carry me. You are too weak right now."

"Of course I can." Bushraal bent down, scooped her up with a grunt, and leaped off the ledge while tightening his grip. He sailed over the battle ground right to the mouth of the cave and set May Lynn down next to Beverly. Olivia crouched and leapt into the air as her wings beat to lift her back up to the landing. She soon returned with Mash.

As Olivia set Mash on the ground, Bushraal spun on his heel and ran into the cave. Olivia also dashed into battle and disappeared. Mash, who had only been sitting for a second, said, "You have got to be kidding me." He pushed himself up and limped after Bushraal.

"Mash, get back here!" screamed Beverly.

Mash ignored her and kept trying to run to catch up with Bush-raal. When he did, he yelled, "Bushraal, what are you doing?"

Bushraal shoved Mash out of the way. "You are not wanted. I do not need your help. I am going to fight. Leave me alone. This is not your fight, russet."

"Yes, it is. I live here, too, Bushraal. If it's your fight, it's mine."

Bushraal growled. "Do whatever you want. Get yourself killed for all I care." Running into battle, he said, "I wish for a bow and arrows and armor." A shiny metal breastplate formed around him, leaving room for the wings that were still at his back. In one hand appeared a bow, and in the other was a fistful of arrows. He drew the bow, and the arrow plunged straight into the face of a monsternite.

Mash went with the old standby of a set of knives and stayed close enough to Bushraal to keep an eye on him but far enough away so that he wouldn't get yelled at. As Mash looked away at an approaching monsternite, Bushraal disappeared. Mash searched for him and spotted him across the room near the tank with King Mermano inside. The tank had been jostled during the battle and had a crack in it and was leaking water. Mash pushed past soldiers and tripped over bodies. Scorso threw Bushraal against the glass tank with his tail, which cracked it even more. Scorso bared his razor-sharp teeth at Bushraal. Bushraal tried to move, but King Mermano's arms behind him came through the glass, which was now more the consistency of a sparklesphere, and grabbed Bushraal by the upper arms, holding him back.

CHAPTER FOURTEEN

"Your majesty? I am trying to help you." Bushraal struggled. The King's eyes were yellow and serpentine, like a monsternite's, instead of blue and clear like they normally were.

Scorso drew his large head back, and the ruffled black feathers on his back settled down against his leathery hide. "You can have your King back. All I want are the visitors. I know you are hiding them somewhere. We found them before with the help your uncle. But you boys have gotten in the way. Not any longer."

"My family is faithful to the kingdom!" Bushraal struggled against the merman's strong grasp.

"Baby soldier, there are ways of convincing everyone. Even your uncle. I thought he would be more useful, but he was so weak even a russet took him out."

"I didn't know—" Mash started, but Scorso cut him off with a roar that made Mash's teeth chatter. With a trembling voice, Mash asked. "What do you want with the visitors? I thought you liked the last one. And since when can monsternites talk?"

"Liked him?" Scorso's voice rolled like powerful waves crashing against an ocean shore. "Shrewtonite." As Scorso said his name, wads of spit flew from his mouth. Mash turned his face away. "Shrewtonite was not a friend of the monsternites. He used us and tortured us when we did not obey. After he ran away, like a coward, I moved into the castle and had a monsternite on guard at all times in case a visitor arrived. I was certain that every passage to the Ama Ranth was in the castle, but I was wrong. And I am the only one who can talk. Shrewtonite taught me that, too."

"We all thought you wanted to take the power from the merpeople, like Shrewtonite wanted."

Scorso stomped a few steps in one direction before stomping back in the other direction. His long body did not allow him to pace very far. "Peace. I want peace for my race."

Bushraal writhed against the King's bulging arms. "These visitors are not like the last. They are peaceful."

"Enough. Shrewtonite was Ned. They all start out that way, but then they change and crave power. I want them eliminated, and I want to do it myself." Addressing the King, he said, "Finish him off. Make it subtle." King Mermano released one of Bushraal's arms and instead reached for his throat. Bushraal tried to pull his hand away, but the King was too strong.

Mash darted away from Scorso and dove at the tank. He drove the blade of one of his knives into a crack in the tank. Bushraal choked as Mash thrust the metal into the crack again and again. Sweat beaded on his forehead as he desperately tried to break the glass.

"I wish for a diamond blade," said Mash. The blade of his knife transformed into a radiating prism of solid diamond. He drove the tip into the damaged part of the tank, and the crack spidered out around the four walls of the tank. Mash kicked the glass, and the tank shattered. Water rushed out, and King Mermano fell to the ground and lost his grip on Bushraal.

Scorso roared and came at Mash with his massive teeth. The puddles that had formed on the ground rippled with every step. Against the dark mountain floor, the water made it look like a tar pit that would suck Mash down into it if he didn't do something. Mash wound up and threw the diamond knife directly at Scorso's heart. Scorso bellowed and crashed into a wall. From the force of Scorso's sharp movements, the knife came loose and flew in Mash's direction.

The blade sliced through the flesh of Mash's leg, and Mash cried out in agony.

Scorso took a few awkward steps and slammed against the cave wall. The soldiers, who had fallen quiet, dodged out of his way to make a path. The only sounds were the thundering stomps from the monsternite's enormous feet and his pained screams. Once outside, the monsternite flapped his giant wings and lifted off the mountainside, but the damage was done. He fell from the sky and crashed into the ground, making the earth shake and creating a crater around himself. The soldiers stared in disbelief. Gradually, they began to care for the wounded and deceased.

As for the monsternites, they left the soldiers alone and flew out of the cave to their individual nesting areas. Without the brains and guidance of Scorso, the search for the visitors was of little interest to the beasts.

After the battle had ended, Beverly and May Lynn, who had stayed at the mouth of cave, found Mash and Bushraal even more disheveled than they had been when they were freed by Olivia. Mash was lying down with one hand pressed against the gash in his thigh and one arm over his forehead. Bushraal sat with his back to Mash and rubbed his throat where the merman had been holding him. King Mermano lay motionless nearby amid a pile of broken glass and a puddle of water.

Olivia ran to the King. "Your majesty!" She put her head near his chest. "He is still breathing. He was under some sort of spell when he hurt Bushraal. I am going to carry him down to the lake."

The panicked expressions of the two girls were the only response to her statement.

"Mash is weak, but he will make it." Olivia's years of experience in battle left her with little sympathy for nonfatal wounds. Handing Beverly a bottle, she said, "Here, give him this. It's for the pain." Beverly took it from her. Lifting the King, who was limp in her arms, Olivia ran back toward the front of the cave.

Beverly went to Mash's side. She held the bottle at arm's length. She removed the cork, took a sniff, and turned her head away. "What is this?" She held up Mash's head, and tipped the bottle over his lips.

Mash drank but then coughed as the liquid burned his throat. Bushraal took the bottle and poured a generous amount on the wound, which made Mash flinch and moan. Beverly winced, and Mash snatched her hand.

Bushraal knelt at Mash's other side, and May Lynn stood behind Bushraal with her hands clasped in front of her chest. Bushraal ripped off the longer sleeve of his shirt and handed it to Beverly. "This is for the bleeding. Apply pressure while I wrap his leg." He ripped off a strip from the bottom of his shirt. Mash shifted. "Do not move. This is going to hurt."

Beverly pressed her hand with the wad of fabric to Mash's leg.

"It does not look very deep." Bushraal wrapped the strips of fabric around the leg and tied them. "Let him rest here for a little while until the bleeding stops, then we will make our journey back to the castle."

Perspiration formed on Mash's forehead, so Beverly ripped off a few leaves from her dress and wiped them across his face.

"I taste metal," whispered Mash. His lips were red with blood.

"We will get some water. And some food," said Bushraal.

Mash turned his head from Beverly to Bushraal. "I'm sorry. I didn't know he was your uncle," he croaked.

"I know. I understand that now. Truthfully, I did not know my uncle. He was estranged from the family, and I would not be surprised if he was working with the monsternites. But he was my father's only brother. He was all that is left of my father's blood."

"Besides you," said Mash.

"Besides me." Bushraal sniffed and wiped his nose with the back of his hand. "I taught you well, russet. You freed the King. You are a hero now. That was some impressive knife slinging until you sliced your own leg open."

Mash tried to laugh, but held onto himself in pain. He moved his hand away from his dirt and blood-streaked face and closed his eyes in pain from the effort of laughing.

Beverly ran a finger across his forehead to move his hair to one side, and he relaxed his face. "You and Bushraal are so brave."

He opened his eyes. "We need to get you home."

Beverly patted his hand. "Take your time, Mash. I want you to feel better first."

CHAPTER FIFTEEN

The castle was mostly abandoned when they passed through its gates again. In the courtyard, someone had broken the head off of the Shrewtonite statue, and the fountain trickled water into the basin. The monsternite and land walker guards on the premises were nowhere to be seen. The few remaining russet workers that hadn't evacuated the moment they heard Scorso was dead wandered around with slumped shoulders and blank faces like they were lost.

The fountain they were seeking was magically back in its original location. The water in the fountain had recovered from being stifled by the sand in the castle. Water bubbled out of the top and splashed down into the pool that had already collected in the basin. The sounds of the gurgling water comforted them, and the four stood in reverent silence for a few moments.

Bushraal held out his elbow to May Lynn, and she wrapped her arm around it. Beverly stood still and kept her eyes trained on the ground until Mash hobbled over to her and swung his arm around her shoulder.

"You never told us what happened after Tumpske locked us in the punishment room," said Mash.

"Oh my gosh, we were so scared," said Beverly. "The door just disappeared, and we didn't know what to do. We ran back to the dining room to try to find help, and May Lynn saw two people she recognized."

"Yeah, those guys you were filling fountains with, Mash. They were walking into the dining room at the same time we were."

Beverly bobbed her head. "We told them everything even though we didn't know if it was the right thing to do."

"I wanted to find Nautica because I remembered she could read your minds. The younger guy...Lontano, right?" asked May Lynn.

"Lonny, yeah," said Mash.

"Lonny said he'd help us find Nautica. She was waiting for us at the river's edge, and she told us you were trapped somewhere in the mountain. But she knew the army was going to attack the next day, so she asked Lonny if Beverly and I could stay with his family for the night."

Beverly interrupted. "Then some guy ran into the room where we were all sleeping and yelled something about a battle going on in the mountain. Everyone was really worried and started freaking out."

May Lynn sighed. "That's when we knew it was time to go. Lonny showed us the way until we found Olivia. And you know the rest."

"Wow, I should let Nautica know I'm safe after this," said Mash.

Bushraal pulled May Lynn's arm a little closer under his elbow. "That was smart of you to go find Nautica."

"With all this fighting, I bet you can't wait to get home," said Mash.

Beverly clutched Mash's waist. "It was the scariest. Even after all that, I kinda don't want to go."

"Don't say that," said Mash. "I would go, if I could. I'll figure out how to get there someday. And then I'll come find you girls." He squeezed Beverly's shoulder. "You." His hand found the back of her neck under her curtain of hair as he pulled her toward him, wrapping his other arm around her back. He felt her hand press into his back, too. He held on tight, wishing there was a way for him to go with her.

Bushraal and May Lynn faced each other with the back of May Lynn's legs leaning on the fountain. They just stared for moments, memorizing each other's faces. "Are you sure you would not want to stay?" asked Bushraal.

"I can't, but if I can come back and visit, I will. All the time," said May Lynn.

Bushraal squeezed both her hands. They embraced and separated to say goodbye to their other traveling companions.

Bushraal and Beverly shared a quick, affectionate hug, and Beverly waved a little before she sat on the edge of the fountain and waited for May Lynn.

"I wasn't sure about you at first, but you really are a good guy. I hope you do make it to our land someday."

"Thank you, May Lynn. That means a lot." Mash gave her a big bear hug, taking her off guard so that she let out a little squeak.

Beverly waded into the water, and Bushraal was quick to offer a hand to help both of the girls in. Once they were standing up to their knees in running water, Beverly asked, "Hey Bushraal, do you think your mom wants these back?" She held up the side of her now-dingy flowery dress.

"No, no, you keep those. Take care, May Lynn and Beverly. Hurry back if you can."

"We will," they said. The girls waved as they stepped backwards to let the water from the highest tier spill over their heads...and then they were gone. Mash leaned his elbow on Bushraal's shoulder, and the boys waved back.

෫෯෫෯෫෯

Bushraal let Mash use his shoulder as a crutch while they walked back to the lake to meet Nautica. They walked in contemplative silence through the castle. It wasn't until they passed through the doors of the courtyard that Mash spoke.

"I give you a lot of credit, Bushraal."

"Graciyoo. Why?"

"I don't know how anyone could be a soldier. To see that much pain and death. And then to know that you probably caused some of that pain and death." Mash shook his head. "I couldn't do it."

Bushraal pondered that for a moment. "You know, I originally only wanted to be a soldier because my father was one. I wanted to be as accomplished a bowman as he was. But it is more than that now. I like protecting people, and I like training people. You, Beverly, and May Lynn helped me learn that. If I have to fight sometimes to protect the freedom of my family and friends, I will do it willingly. And then someday, after I am no longer a recruit myself, I can train new recruits."

"You would be good at that, as much as I hate to admit it."

"If I can train you, I can train anyone."

Mash didn't argue. "I was pretty hopeless, wasn't I?"

Bushraal just laughed through his nose in response. "What are you plans?"

"You mean besides getting out of here as soon as I can?"

"Yes, besides that."

Mash rolled his shoulders and adjusted his grip on Bushraal's. "I think I'll take up the family business, too. I like talking to people and keeping a journal. It's the best fit for me while I'm still here."

Bushraal nodded.

Only Nautica's forehead and vibrant blue orbs peeked above the water as the boys approached.

"What were you doing?" asked Mash.

Her pale green finger appeared above the surface to point behind them. In the distance, a monsternite circled one of the mountains before disappearing behind it. When she was sure it was safe, she propelled her entire torso out of the water with a push of her tail, grabbed Mash and Bushraal by the waists of their shorts, and pulled them into the lake with two big splashes. Mash sputtered and flailed while he treaded water with his good leg.

"Do not ever get yourselves captured like that again!" She embraced them both around the neck in more of a headlock than a hug. "I was so worried."

"Chill out, Nautica," said Mash.

"Yes, please. I have already been choked once today," said Bushraal.

She released them. "Sorry."

Bushraal felt his neck where it was still red from the King's hold. "It is alright. Thank you for your concern." He paddled to the shore. "I should get home to my mother."

"Will you visit me?" She batted her eyes at Bushraal.

He bowed his head. "As often as I can."

Nautica's green cheeks turned pink.

Bushraal offered Mash a hand as Mash crawled onto the shore. Then, they faced each other, put a hand over their own hearts, and nodded.

"Let me know when your next quest is. I will write all about it," said Mash.

Bushraal smiled. "I shall." He stomped off toward the tree line.

❧❧❧

The pace was slow with Mash limping along next to the water. He located a large stick lying on the ground that looked like the one he had used the day he met Bushraal. With the stick helping him walk, he was able to keep up a little better. Nautica seemed pleased with the slow progression after having to rush back and forth the past couple days. It almost felt like a normal day with Nautica and Mash taking a walk together and making fun of each other.

Except everything had changed. They had seen death and torture and hunger. And Nautica no longer felt the need to flirt with Mash. Instead of the wistful glances directed at him, they were now directed far off into the distance, perhaps thinking about Bushraal. But Mash didn't mind. Behind his own wistful glances were thoughts of the other land, even more enthusiastic than ever.

After some time, what was left of Mash's house became visible on the horizon. He came to a halt and leaned on his walking stick. "What if my parents aren't there?"

"They are."

Nautica's eyes watered, but no tears fell. "They have been waiting for you."

"I will come visit you tomorrow. I want to hear all about everything you did while I was locked in that cell. Will you be alright without me the rest of the way?"

Nautica scoffed. "Yes, I think I will manage, gimpy. I will see you tomorrow." Mash shot her one of his sideways grins and headed off toward his house in the distance.

His mother must've seen him coming because she was running toward him before he was anywhere near the house. Far away, he could see his father standing in front of their tree home. His mother sobbed. Mash quickened his pace and dropped the stick before they reached each other. Then she held him in her arms and patted his head as she cried into his hair. "I thought you had gone to the Ama Ranth. You look thinner. And your leg. What happened to your leg?"

Mash rubbed his mother's back. "I promised I wouldn't go. I will tell you and father the whole story if you can wish me up something to eat and drink. And maybe if I can sleep on your bed tonight."

"Of course, Son. Whatever you want." She squeezed his shoulders the whole walk back to the house.

His father with his angular features, which Mash resembled a little more now, smiled the same crooked smile. "You're a hero, Son." He gave Mash a big bear hug. "I wish I could have been there with you."

"No, you don't. Trust me. But I wish you were there, too, Dad." They went inside and Mash opted to lie on his parents' bed while devouring every kind of food his parents could wish up while he recounted the entire story to them.

CHAPTER SIXTEEN

"Mash, go find a sparklesphere, I have a surprise for you." Mash had just stripped his shirt off and was about to jump in the lake for a swim before Nautica stopped him.

"I can't just swim there?" he asked. "Must be some surprise."

"It is."

It had been almost a year since Beverly and May Lynn had come to Flowerantha. The monsternites had dispersed and only descended their mountain when they needed to feed. Mash still longed to go to the other land and had almost nightly dreams about Beverly, May Lynn, and where they came from. But he tried to stay busy. He had begun to go to work with his father, absorbing everything the people reported; and in his free time, he would swim with Nautica or bother Bushraal on his quests.

Mash dove into the water and opened his eyes underwater in search of a sparklesphere. He bobbed to the top and moved one into position. Mash climbed into the sparklesphere and Nautica pushed it toward the middle of the lake. "Where are we headed? Visiting Olivia? Maybe saying hi to the King and Queen?"

"No, not quite." She pushed the sphere deep into the water away from where the palace was located. On the floor of the lake, Nautica released the sparklesphere for a second so that it hovered right above a bed of rainbow-colored coral. When Nautica swam through the coral, it separated to let her pass. When the coral parted, a cave appeared behind it.

"What is this? Some kind of hide out? I like how hidden it is."

"Mash, brace yourself."

"I'm in a sparklesphere, Nautica. What could I possibly do?"

She was smiling, but the smile did not reach her large, glassy eyes. "They found a portal to the Ama Ranth. This isn't a cave. It's the passageway."

A toothy, open-mouthed grin formed on Mash's face. "No way."

Nautica breathed a laugh. "It is true. Volunteer merpeople have been testing it for days." Mash stared at the cave. "There is only one problem. Only one mermaid has returned. All but one of the volunteers are still swimming around somewhere in the Ama Ranth. So if you go, there is no guarantee that you can come back."

"I've always understood that." He placed his hands against the inside of the sparklesphere and pressed his nose up to its springy surface.

"I know," said Nautica. "I just wanted to make sure."

"You should come, too." Nautica shook her head. "But now that there are other mermaids there, you won't be alone. And I'll make sure I live near the water to keep an eye on you."

"Mash, I am staying. But you should go." Nautica helped him by pushing the sparklesphere near the mouth of the cave.

"Take care of Bushraal," said Mash. "And make sure he takes care of you. Remember that you can do better than that wannabe soldier."

"Mash."

"I'm kidding."

"I know. Are you ready?"

"One more thing. Will you let my parents know where I've gone?"

Nautica nodded. "Of course."

"Try to be gentle with my mother. She won't be happy about it." Tears pricked Mash's eyes, but he didn't let any fall.

"I will."

Mash stuck his arms out of the sparklesphere, and Nautica pulled him out into the open water. She embraced him and kissed him on the cheek, and then pulled his arm to the opening of the cave. He waved before he backed into the moving water with shoots of rainbow colors going through it. And then all he could see were the colors—orange, yellow, green, blue, and pink. And then there was air and sand and children playing and buildings. He had made it.

EPILOGUE

With the water obscuring their vision, beams of color appeared. The ground fell out underneath them, and they slid down a chute of colors—orange, yellow, green, blue, and pink. No dark purple. Although they were under the water, they did not get wet except for their legs submerged in the fountain. The colors subsided, and the girls landed on wet grass. A clear stream of water sprinkled on their heads.

The sun blinded Beverly, and she closed one of her eyes. "We're back."

"What are you guys wearing?" a voice asked. Beverly's older brother Rob had a basketball in the crook of his elbow and was headed to May Lynn's front yard to play on their hoop. The girls scrambled up to get out of the water as Rob approached.

"We're uh, pretending."

"To be what?"

"Mermaids," said May Lynn. "Mermaid princesses."

"Weird," he said and walked away.

Beverly pulled her dress off so that she was just wearing her swimsuit again. "There, now we can avoid any other questions."

May Lynn did the same. "What are you going to do with your dress?"

Beverly bunched hers up while May Lynn carefully creased and folded hers. "I don't know. Hang it in my closet and stare at it. Or plant it in the garden. Maybe lend it to you some day as a hand-me-down." She crinkled her nose, and May Lynn giggled.

Continue the adventure with *Olivia's Story*, part of the *People of Flowerantha* series of short stories

Olivia's current mission, if she chose to accept it, which she always did, was to escort four children and a mermaid. But these weren't all normal Floweranthan children. Two of the children were from the *Ama Ranth*, the other land, which is why the mission appealed to her. She had to help two overenthusiastic boys and their mermaid friend return the two girls to the Ama Ranth. It should be fairly straightforward as long as the *monsternites*, giant winged beasts, stayed out of their way. Having the mermaid along complicated things because she could be a meal for the monsternites.

Olivia kicked her webbed feet and pushed the door open to her home—a small alcove just outside of the merpalace. Olivia worked as the go-between for the land walkers and sea dwellers, but she also attended to any random task that the King and Queen needed fulfilled, which meant that they always liked her to be close by.

King Mermano and Queen Mermaida had given her a room in the palace—a glorious room with every comfort imaginable—but Olivia did not spend much time in that room. Only when she needed to spend days in the palace would she use her opulent, royal bedroom. Her alcove was a better location, and she could leave at a moment's notice at any sign of trouble. Her room in the underwater palace required her to go down too many corridors and talk to too many merpeople. It wasn't that Olivia didn't enjoy conversing with the merpeople—she wanted to protect each and every one—but she loved efficiency more.

Olivia's silvery hair reached down to her backside, and she braided it to keep it out of the way. Underwater, she didn't bother with clothes as most of her body was covered in shimmery greenish gray scales, but she kept battle armor and two dresses made out of a quick-drying spongy material in a trunk in her alcove for when she needed to do business on land.

She eased onto the large, dense sponge she used as a chair and gingerly lifted a seaweed patch that was wrapped around her shoulder. She winced. The gash was deep, but it was not bleeding like it had been. Although monsternites had not bothered the land walkers in recent years unless they got in the way, the beasts had a fondness for the occasional mermaid snack. Since Olivia was half mermaid, they settled for her. Monsternites weren't as dumb as they looked, and this particular one had almost taken a bite out of Olivia while she was trying to protect a school of merchildren.

She replaced the seaweed. She shouldn't complain about the pain. She wouldn't let any of the soldiers complain, so she couldn't either. Her eyes wandered in search of something to take her mind off the nuisance.

Against one wall of her bedroom was a massive sheet of canvas with the names of the royal court, soldiers, and staff, even including the people who prepared royal feasts. Olivia first stared at the list from a distance, taking in the whole expanse of names at once. Then, she inspected it closer, running her finger down a column of names. Using a quill filled with squid ink, she added the names, "Bushraal," "Mash," and "Nautica" to the bottom of the list. They were now official members of the royal staff, in her mind.

Olivia reclined on her bed and drifted off to sleep as she gazed at the list of names. The next day should be an easy one. She didn't anticipate any complications while walking children across Flowerantha. She slept peacefully that night and dreamt about the banquet that would be prepared when she would announce that the visitors were here and gone, and then her life would return to normal.

Read it for free at https://books2read.com/u/bzpgMD!

ACKNOWLEDGMENTS

This story has come a long way from where it began thanks to my insightful beta readers, Jill, Leslie, and Malinda. Jill and Leslie, thank you for giving me some great feedback on my scattered, unfocused early drafts. Malinda, fantasy genre expert, I very much appreciate all your guidance and ideas. And horse knowledge. All three of you helped me hone in on the strongest storyline and point of view. Rebecca, I appreciate your expert advice so much. Your ideas elevated Flowerantha, and your encouragement helped propel me to finally finish the darn thing. Mom, thank you again for your careful proofreading. Now I know where I got all my editorial skills from. Wink. Leslie, thank you so much for your beautiful artwork, making Mash come to life. And thank you to Katie for making my cover look pretty. Also, hey to my local ladies! It's so nice having other writers around to commiserate and celebrate with. Thanks for all the fun write-ins! Here's to many more together. Finally, I could not and would not have done this without the NaNoWriMo challenge and the support and camaraderie of the Nano community.

GLOSSARY

Ama Ranth: other land, where May Lynn and Beverly come from

aquasus: a horse with wings and hooves that transform into webbed feet, like a duck's, when they touch water

brine pool: a large area of salt on the ocean floor, which creates a pool. In Flowerantha, it is used by the royal family as a way to see all of their subjects.

cerulean: hello

deraino: you're welcome

donch coilee: dark purple

erosea: I love you

gaff: a curse word in Floweranthan

gamboge: a fast-moving sloth with white hair and a yellow snout

graciyoo: thank you

maoompy: an exclamation that expresses disgust

monsternite: a Tyrannosaurus Rex with wings and feathers

russet: a peasant, commoner, or poor person

sparklesphere: flexible, oblong bubbles that land walkers use for transportation in water

zomp: a creature that resembles an alien and is known for playing tricks on people

ABOUT BEK CASTRO

Rebekah N. Bryan, also known as Bek Castro, was born in Columbus, Wisconsin, and graduated from the University of Wisconsin–Whitewater. She currently works as a technical writer and lives near Milwaukee with her husband and two children.

Join Bek's mailing list to be the first to hear about new projects.
http://eepurl.com/bqj2a9

Visit http://www.rebekahnbryan.com for the latest news.
Like Bek on Facebook: https://www.facebook.com/rebekahnbryan
Follow Bek on Twitter: https://twitter.com/rebekahnbryan

Made in the USA
Charleston, SC
10 March 2017